MIDI

Copyright © 2024 by Loni Ree

All rights reserved. No part of this book may be reproduced in any form or by any electronic or mechanical means, including information storage and retrieval systems, without written permission from the author, except for the use of brief quotations in a book review.

Please respect the author and do not participate in or encourage piracy of copyrighted materials that would violate the author's rights.

This is a work of fiction. Names, characters, businesses, places, events, locales, and incidents are either the products of the author's imagination or used in a fictitious manner. Any resemblance to actual persons, living or dead, or actual events is purely coincidental.

Edited By: Kendra's Editing and Book Services

Cover Design By: Bookinit Designs

MIDNIGHT FALLS
Texas

Welcome to Midnight Falls, Texas, the small town that's big on Halloween. Literally. Around here, the festivities don't end. But finding forever in a town big on scares hasn't been easy for the lovelorn residents. Until now.

This Halloween, everything changes. Love is in the air, and these matches were written in the stars. All these hunky alphas have to do to claim their spooky-ever-after is prove themselves worthy of the sassy women who drive them wild. No love potions, spells, or magic needed.

Check out the Midnight Falls, Texas series

Midnight Confessions by Tory Baker My Book

Midnight Lessons by Violet Rae

Midnight Treat by Loni Ree

Midnight Masquerade by Nichole Rose

Midnight Rebel by Fern Fraser

Midnight Snack by Kat Baxter

Get How to Love A Heartbreaker FREE when you subscribe to my newsletter!

Loni Ree Romance Newsletter

MIDNIGHT FALLS
Texas

MIDNIGHT
Treat

USA TODAY BESTSELLING AUTHOR
LONI REE

CONTENTS

1. Romi — 11
2. Sullivan — 17
3. Romi — 23
4. Sullivan — 33
5. Romi — 41
6. Sullivan — 49
7. Sullivan — 55
8. Romi — 63
9. Sullivan — 69
10. Romi — 79
11. Sullivan — 87
12. Romi — 93
13. Sullivan — 101
    Epilogue — 109

Related Stories — 115
Subscribe to my Newsletter — 119
Buy Paperbacks and Ebooks — 121
Join my Reader's Group — 123
About the Author — 125
Also by Loni Ree — 127

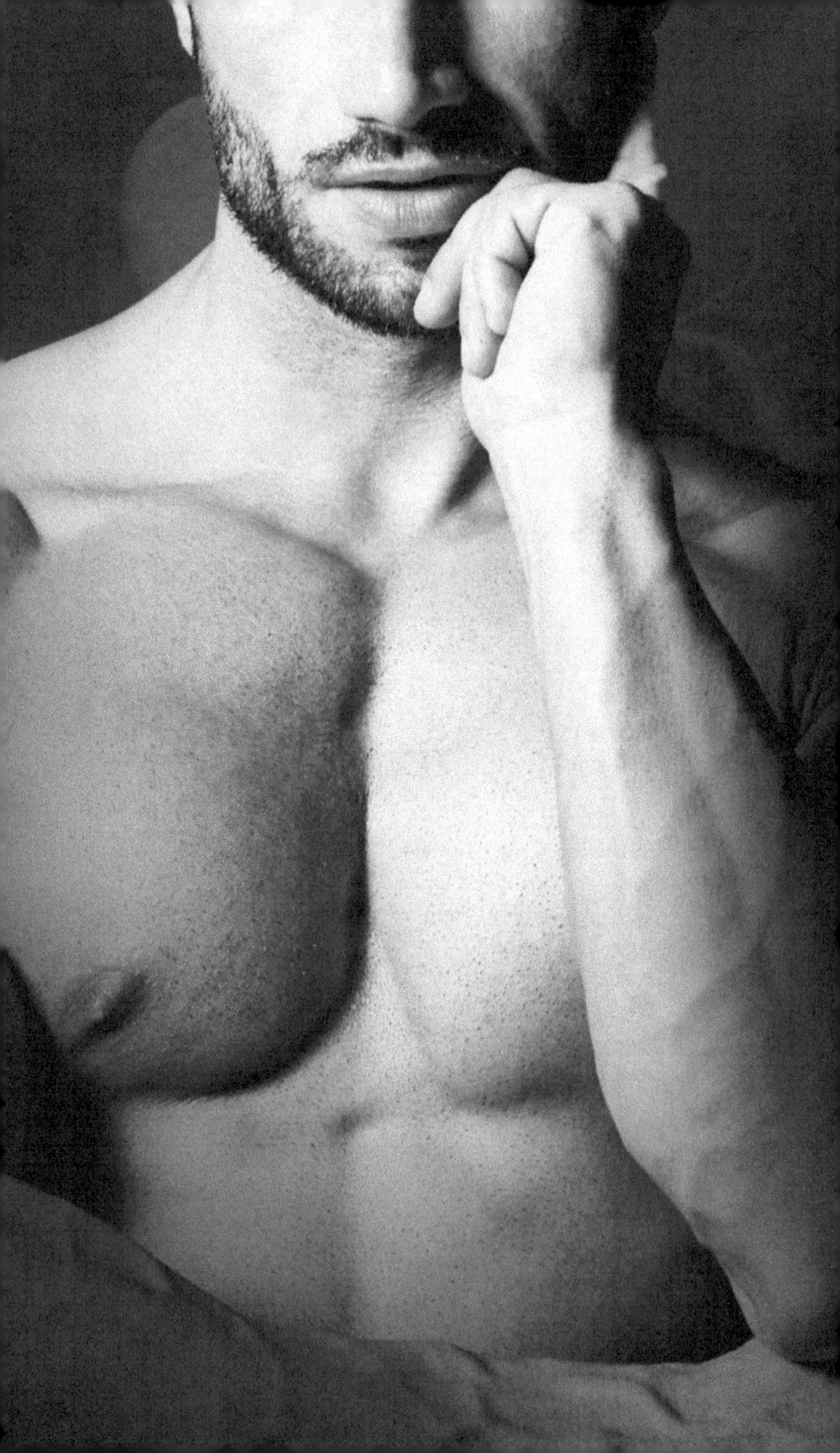

CHAPTER 1
ROMI

In the dimly lit back office of Trick or Treat, I'm sorting through an alarming stack of invoices and receipts because it's just about time to pay the Piper—I mean, the distributor. The office, which I graciously refer to as my lair, is decked out with cobwebs, plastic spiders, and a towering pile of pumpkin-scented candles. It's Halloween central back here, and I wouldn't have it any other way.

Tonight marks the second night of our Thirteen Nights of Halloween celebration at the only bar that could make Tim Burton's dreams look like a half-hearted attempt at being spooky.

In Midnight Falls, Texas, the residents know how to celebrate Halloween like it's a second religion, and Tony, our illustrious owner and former "let's not talk about it" kind of guy, is the mastermind behind it all.

I'm mid-tally of our ghost-themed tequila shots from last night, which were a raging success if the empty bottles of tequila in the recycle bin are anything to go by, when a familiar, gravelly voice wades into my kingdom of clutter and candied chaos.

"Good afternoon! Need a hand with the daily paperwork hell?"

Tony, the big boss with a voice that can charm or threaten depending on his mood and a smile that says he's up to no good, stands there in the doorway. His massive frame casts an almost theatrical shadow. I'd bet a month's salary that the leather jacket he's wearing costs more than my car. He's got that classic Godfather grin, and I can't help but smirk back.

"Not at all. I'm actually almost done," I quip, swirling a pen like a wand.

He lets out a hearty laugh, the kind that rumbles through the room like distant thunder. "Great."

Tony saunters in, taking a moment to glance around at the Halloween paraphernalia that looks like it had a few too many shots itself and exploded all over the room.

"I see you've been busy making this place look like a witch's den," he says, eyeing a particularly large rubber bat hanging from the ceiling. It swoops down every time the door opens, which, in my mind, is the perfect greeting.

"It's called ambiance. And maybe a little warning to the employees not to mess with me."

Tony chuckles, settling into one of the sturdy leather chairs opposite my desk.

"Just making sure my star manager doesn't need anything before the nightly festivities begin. Also, you know, making sure you're still standing after last night. I heard Scooter and Brenda started a 'Thriller' flash mob on the dance floor last night." Those two regulars are always ready to add to the mayhem.

"Well, Scooter's definitely something at the moonwalk, and Brenda managed to turn it into a two-step halfway through. They kept the slightly plastered crowd entertained, though I suspect the allure was more about how long they'd stay upright."

Tony nods appreciatively, rubbing his chin like a proud dad. "Our Halloween extravaganza is already the most popular event in town."

"In a town that celebrates Halloween year-round, we couldn't lose," I add. "Especially with the costume contests and that 'Bobbing for Bloody Marys' game you dreamed up. Add in the haunted speakeasy hidden behind the floor-to-ceiling bookcase and you've got the perfect combination for this town."

Tony glances over at me and asks, "What about you? How are you holding up with all the craziness?"

"So far, so good, but I might have a different opinion once Halloween is over. I might need an extra day or two off the first week of November to recover."

"Consider it done," Tony says, getting up from the antique chair with surprising grace. "Let me know if anything changes. Oh, and don't forget about the ax juggling contest tomorrow." He shakes his head like he's still a little shocked we managed to talk him into the crazy stunt. We hired professional jugglers and a horror movie special effects designer to make sure the event is one to remember. Of course, none of our patrons are aware it's all staged.

"I'll save you a spot," I tease, watching him retreat back toward the haunted cacophony of Trick or Treat's frontlines.

"That won't be necessary. Just let me know when it's over."

Once I wade my way through the paperwork catastrophe, I decide to check out the main bar and make sure everything is going okay since the bar opened an hour ago. While I love my bat-cave lair, out there is where the magic-slash-pandemonium happens.

The bar is as packed as ever. There's a medley of witches, vampires, and what looks disturbingly like an off-brand Joker blending humor and chaos. It's only eight pm, but the partying is in full force.

And there, in the middle of it all, is my team, orchestrating the chaos beautifully. Shane, the head bartender, is doing his best zombie bartender impression, complete with a 'need brains, have beer' apron. Shana, the head server who moonlights as the queen of mischief, is adding the final touches to what could best be described as a creepy carnival setup.

"Hey, Romi!" Shana calls, drawing me over. "You're gonna love this. We managed to get the ancient fog machine we found in the storage room set up so it looks like the drinks are floating through a cemetery."

"Brilliant." I grin, taking in the sight of wispy clouds rolling along the bar top. "They go perfect with the glow-in-the-dark tombstones."

"Here's your poison." Shane hands me my usual Diet Coke with a splash of cherry syrup.

"Thank you," I call over my shoulder as I wander over toward the stage where tonight's karaoke monsters are lining up.

It's nights like these I love most, even if it means less sleep and more challenges. What other job lets you mix goblins with martinis and get paid for it? Tony often jokes that if his former job had this many costumes and candy corn, he might never have switched over.

As the night rolls on, I remember why our quirky town of Midnight Falls feels like home. It's more than the full-moon weirdness or the jack-o'-lantern streetlamps. It's this—people coming together, pouring into Tony's grand vision with a dash of my offbeat management style. A place where even ghosts can order a pint.

By closing time, I've lost count of the karaoke vampires serenading the room with off-key renditions of 'Monster Mash'. I have the best job ever!

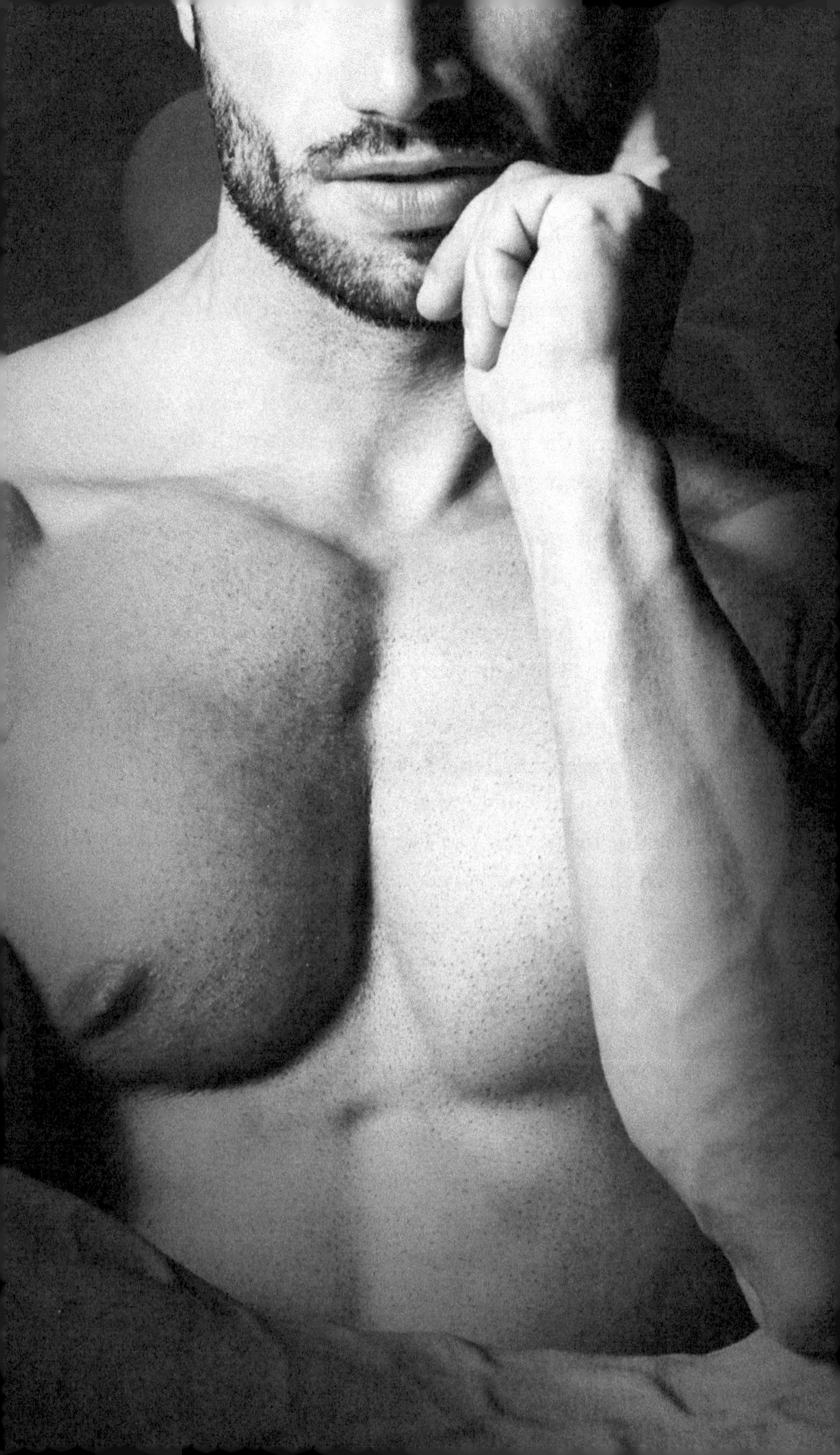

CHAPTER 2
SULLIVAN

The past week has been a whirlwind of animatronic arms moving when they shouldn't and smoke machines that seemed to have a mind of their own. I'm still surprised no one has summoned an actual ghost from the eerie atmosphere we've been conjuring. But at long last, "The Reaper's Reckoning" ride is up and running, terrorizing visitors just the way it's meant to and without any unintended asphyxiation events. With that checked off the list, I'm itching for a change of scenery.

So tonight, I've traded the techno-haunts for Trick or Treat, the newly minted bar that everyone in Midnight Falls is raving about. The thrilling bar is deep into its Thirteen Nights of Halloween celebration, and I'm game to join the fun. Who needs an excuse to don vampire garb in a town that reveres Halloween as devoutly as Texans do barbecue?

As I approach the bar, confidently swishing my ridiculous cape, I spot Hugh, the high school wrestling coach who moonlights as a bouncer, at the bar. He's decked out in a snug T-rex costume. Irony at its finest since the guy could intimidate a rock if he chose.

"Evening, Count Sullivan," he greets me with a chuckle, his roar more purr at this point in the evening. "Here for a couple of pints of Type O?"

"Definitely if you've got it on draft," I quip back, biting down a grin. Hugh and I swap a few more playful jabs about fangs and fossils before he steps aside to let me in.

The interior of Trick or Treat is everything I've been told. The vintage stained-glass windows that line all the walls display scenes of autumn landscapes and Halloween motifs. When the disco lights hit them, they cast vibrant hues throughout the room, infusing the space with the festive spirit of this unique town. Each pane seems to narrate its own tale of artistry combined with spookiness.

Stretching across the far wall of the bar is a stunning stained-glass mural that intricately depicts spooky Halloween scenes. The rich colors of the glass send prismatic patterns through the room, creating a kaleidoscope of shadows and light that breathes life into the mystical scene.

There are several gothic-style fireplaces throughout the bar, their stone mantels adorned with gargoyles and twisted vines. These fireplaces cast a warm, inviting glow that complements the flickering candlelight scattered throughout the bar. The gentle crackle of burning embers adds a comforting sound to the ambiance.

Above us, elaborate chandeliers hang gracefully over all three levels of the bar, each a masterpiece of wrought iron and crystal. Shaped like upside-down black roses, their glossy petals cradle soft lights that cast intricate patterns on the ceiling and floors. As they sway slightly, the crystals catch the light, creating a dazzling effect that mimics twinkling stars in an inky night sky.

Three levels make up the bar, connected by sweeping wrought iron staircases adorned with carved pumpkins and trailing ivy. From the upper levels, you get a bird's eye view of the bustling crowd below, each patron enveloped in Trick or Treat's enchanting, ghostly charm. It's a seamless blend of whimsy and gothic style, fusing Halloween mystery with vintage elegance.

But what truly intrigues visitors are the whispers about what's hidden beneath the main floor. Rumor has it there's a unique speakeasy in the abandoned bomb shelter below the bar.

Known as Scared Shotless, this exclusive, invitation-only haunt is accessed through a secret door tucked behind an ordinary bookcase. Supposedly, the speakeasy boasts a Prohibition-era vibe, complete with vintage furnishings and a menu of classic, handcrafted cocktails.

As I glance around the crowded room, my eyes are immediately drawn to a Cher look-alike behind the bar, serving drinks like she's performing at Madison Square Garden. She's a tiny little thing, curvy in all the right ways, and judging by her no-nonsense demeanor, she knows how to work a room, or haunt in this case. With her long jet-black hair tied back into an uncomplicated ponytail, she somehow embodies the rock star glam with an effortless flair.

I saunter up to the bar, channeling centuries-old charm. "Can I get a Blood Mary?" I flash what I hope is a dazzling, fangy smile.

Without skipping a beat, she glances at me with something between amused tolerance and mild exasperation. "The other bartender will be here to take your order shortly," she says in a rich, velvety voice that does all sorts of interesting things to my internal organs and one external organ. What the fuck?

Before I can form a coherent sentence, she pivots, ponytail swinging, and disappears into the throng like it's Houdini Night. Oh, no, little goddess, you aren't getting away that easily.

Not to be thwarted by a high-heeled retreat, I decide I'm far too interested in this enigma of a woman to just let her disappear. Without stopping to consider my actions, I follow her through the crowd, spotting her slipping down a long hallway that I assume leads to the back.

I hasten my pace, my cape doing its level best to trip me, until I arrive outside a storeroom where I find her muttering to herself while she digs through a large cardboard box.

Stepping into the room, I accidentally kick over a box of black plastic bats. As the black toys spill out across the shiny, treated-concrete floor, she spins around, eyes wide, a startle running through her like she's ready to either scream or throw a novelty skeleton at me.

"Fuck a duck! Are you trying to give me a freaking heart attack?" she gasps, clutching a plastic skull as though it's a makeshift weapon.

"Whoa, sorry!" I raise my hands in mock surrender, wondering why I'm fucking this up so badly. One look at her and I turned into a dipshit with no common sense and two left feet. "No, I was trying to talk to you when you walked away."

Her expression shifts from shocked to deadpan, and there's something about the way she composes herself and glares at me that causes my cock to turn rock hard. "Excuse me." She throws her hands down on her luscious hips and lifts her adorable chin. "You should've gotten the hint that me walking away meant I'm busy and don't have time to talk."

In for a penny, in for a pound. "I figured it meant I had to try harder," I counter, flashing the charming grin I use to get my ass out of tight spots. "So, here I am."

She looks at me for a long moment, deciding whether or not this earns me the right to stay. The challenge in her eyes causes my blood to heat. I'm not sure if I want to spank her ass or kiss her and beg for forgiveness.

"You're in the *employees-only* part of the bar." I guess she isn't in a forgiving mood. "So, Mr. *I Didn't Get the Message The First Time*, what can I do for you, besides not calling security?"

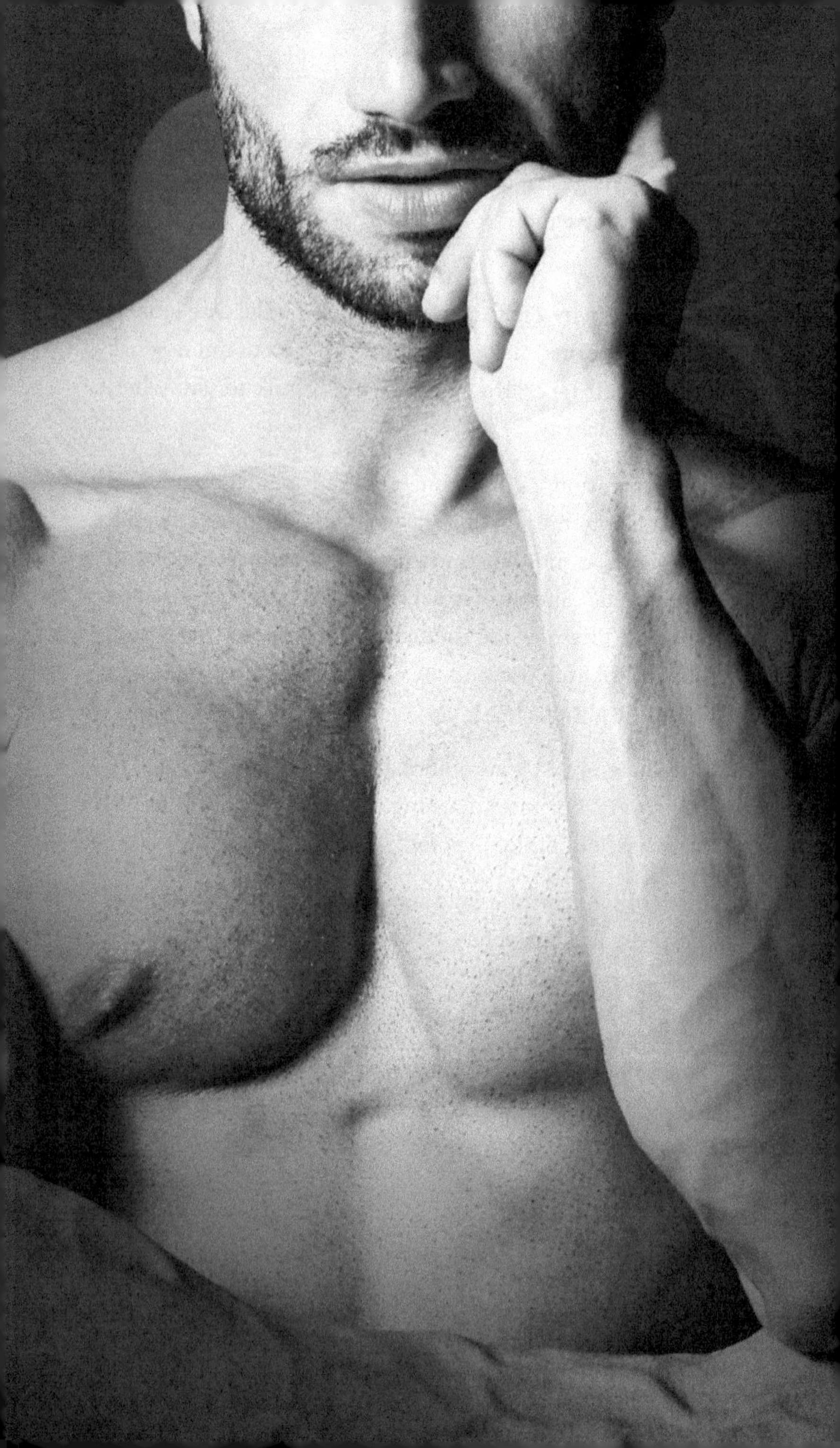

CHAPTER 3
ROMI

Raising his hands in mock surrender, he steps back and flashes his freaking panty-melting grin again. "How about we start over?" There's a pause as if he's giving me the chance to reject his offer.

I narrow my eyes, trying to size him up. Somewhere in the corner of my mind, I acknowledge how tall he is, how his dark hair looks effortlessly tousled, and how that well-trimmed beard would feel rubbing against my inner thighs. Huh? When did I start having crazy thoughts like those? Oh, yeah. The moment the hot vampire with the roguish grin walked into Trick or Treat.

When he says, "I'm Sullivan Midnight," like it's his get-out-of-jail-free card, I groan to myself. Just freaking great. Because what else could add the proverbial cherry to my sundae of chaotic evenings than realizing he's one of those Midnights?

As in the family with their name stamped all over this town and a mansion larger than life sitting on the edge of it like a testament to their power and influence.

Quickly flipping through the mental file of 'Who's Who in Midnight Falls,' I can't help but paste a fake smile on my face. "Sullivan? It must have been a long, painful labor for your mother to come up with that one." Holy smokes. Did that really come out of my mouth? My mouth filter must've gotten fried along with my brain circuits when he walked into the bar.

His deep, genuine laughter shouldn't be as arousing as it is. "Funny, but I'm actually named after my Great Uncle Sullivan."

"Oh, right," I shoot back and tap my forefinger on my chin, remembering some of the town's illustrious past. "Was that the uncle who went crazy and thought he'd been abducted by aliens? I heard he ran through town with a tinfoil hat on his head and not much else."

His eyes crinkle with amusement, apparently enjoying this little exchange more than I anticipated. "No, that was Great Uncle Linus. Great Uncle Sullivan was the one who donated the land for the town library and paid for his brother's therapy."

Why the heck is he so darn intriguing? My stupid girly bits are singing halleluiahs while my heart beats in a funny rhythm.

I exhale, leaning back against the shelves for a modicum of support. It's a precarious fortress built on werewolf shot glasses and ceramic pumpkins. "Alright, Sullivan Midnight, what exactly do you want?"

"To get to know the woman who works in this delightful madhouse," he says, gesturing around as if to emphasize the bar's full-scale animated madness. "You could start by telling me your name."

"Why do you need to know my name?" What can I say? I was born to argue.

"Because I want to get to know you." The arrogant grin slips a little, and I'm pretty sure I heard his back teeth snap together.

"My name is Romi."

"Romi?" He blinks several times. "That's an unusual name. Is that short for something?"

"It's short for none of your business." I glare back at him, unwilling to give even an inch as the little voice in the back of my mind warns me my life will never be the same again.

The words hang in the air between us, mingling with the scent of spiced rum and the dusty nostalgia of faux cobwebs. "What if I want to make it my business?" He steps close enough for me to get a whiff of his yummy, spicy scent. My darn hussy girly bits melt into a pile of goo.

It's like we have an invisible force pulling us together. His arms wrap around me and I blink up in surprise as he leans down toward me. As his warm, soft lips cover mine, my freaking brain shuts down completely while my hussy girly parts run the show. Before I know it, I'm wrapped around him like a boa constrictor.

I return his kisses eagerly, and before I'm able to stop myself, I pull his white dress shirt free of his black pants and slide my hands under it. His back muscles ripple under my touch, encouraging me to continue my exploration.

"Goddamn," he growls against my lips. "I can't get enough of you."

"Then shut up and kiss me again." I can't believe I just ordered this man to keep kissing me in the work stockroom where anyone could walk in.

"Fucking hell." He lifts me up against his hard body and sets me down on the edge of the wooden counter.

There's something grounding about the solid firmness beneath me, juxtaposed with the absolute chaos he's causing within.

My legs spread a little wider, allowing him to step closer, to settle himself between them. It's a sensation both scandalous and perfectly natural. I forget all about the risk to my job and to my heart and fall headfirst into his kiss.

The world around us dissolves until it's just the two of us, caught up in a pulse of shared breath and beating hearts. His hands find a comfortable grip on my waist, and I can feel the warmth of his skin through the thin polyester fabric of my costume.

Right now, I'm convinced that Sullivan Midnight might just be the most dangerous kind of drug in existence. The type who redefines reality, leaving you floating somewhere between fantasy and delirium and completely freaking addicted. All he's done is kiss me, but somehow, that simple act feels more profound than any spell, potion, or séance.

For a second, I genuinely forget how to breathe. Like, I'm pretty sure air is meant to be a fundamental part of continuing to live, but when he kisses me like this, those silly bodily essentials become secondary to Sullivan's magic.

I focus everything on him—the nuances of how each contact of our lips changes and the way he tastes like something smoky like the most expensive whiskey. My hands are clutching his shoulders, perhaps holding on a bit too tightly, but the way he emits a growly pleased rumble in response only encourages me to continue.

When he finally pulls back, I blink up at him, dazed and breathless. His eyes, those brilliant sapphires, are locked onto mine with an intensity that could rival any candlelit confession. "Well, fuck," he murmurs, shock coloring his voice.

"You can say that again," I manage to say, though it comes out sounding a tad airy. I feel like I'm one of those cartoon characters with birds flying around their heads.

He laughs softly, a sound that seems to wrap around me like a comforting blanket, equal parts warmth and desire. "Fuck, fuck, fuck," Sullivan counters, his forehead leaning gently against mine. "I'm glad we're on the same goddamn page."

"Same page? We might be on the same paragraph or sentence," I respond, without considering what I'm saying. "Though I'm a little fuzzy on the punctuation."

"Well, semicolons are for when you're not quite sure what else to use," he jokes, his fingers caressing small soothing circles into my hips, keeping me tethered to the moment.

He kisses me again, softer this time, and my legs curl gently around him, pulling him closer. I feel the hardness of his cock pressed against my girly parts and nearly self-combust on the spot.

Every good sense I've ever had is drowning in the intoxicating pull of Sullivan's kiss. He's standing between my spread legs, drawing me closer like gravity is a practical joke the universe is playing on us both.

Our shared oxygen is a tangible thread, weaving us together in this quiet corner of the world that's momentarily ours. My fingers knot in his hair, dragging his lips impossibly closer. I'm pretty sure my heart's forgotten every beat that isn't in sync with his.

Like a record scratching to a halt, there's a noise in the hallway outside the stockroom. It's nothing more than a clatter, probably just Shane grabbing bottles of liquor, but it's jarring enough to yank me from the magic of the moment.

Reality crashes through me, and panic jolts through my veins.

Abruptly, I pull away from Sullivan. His lips are warm and inviting, so it takes an enormous effort to break the connection. He's left blinking at me with those mesmerizing, blazing blue eyes, a layer of confusion quickly warming them.

"Romi..." His voice trails off as he sees the horror written all over my face.

"I'm... I'm sorry," I stammer, the words tumbling out before they solidify in my brain. Somewhere, deep down, there's worry about jeopardizing my job, my carefully guarded heart, and every other precious thing I've arranged in this precarious balance.

Before he can react, I slide off the counter and cast Sullivan a hasty, apologetic glance before darting out of the stockroom, leaving him standing there, probably as bewildered as I feel.

My mind is an electric storm of thoughts, each bolt striking with enough power to split the precariously balanced composure I'm clinging to. The hallway is a blur as I race down it toward my office, frantically praying I don't run into my boss or anyone else.

I slip inside and shut the door behind me, leaning my back against its sturdy reassurance. It's a small space filled with the comforting chaos of ledgers, order forms, and an old chair that squeaks its indignation at every slight move. Here, I'm safe from the pull of Sullivan's allure and those damnable kisses that threaten to unravel me like a spool of thread spinning wildly out of control.

I dive headfirst into spreadsheets and schedules, anything to keep my mind from spinning back to his lips and hands. And the hardness that both scared and excited my girly parts.

Stop thinking about him, I order myself as numbers jumble and distort. The busier I stay, the less chance there is for memories to overtake me.

I imagine Sullivan out there somewhere in the bar looking for me, trying to piece together the reasons for my hasty retreat.

A part of me wants him to storm in here, demanding to know what the hell just happened, and a more terrifying part of me knows I'd probably make a fool of myself if he did.

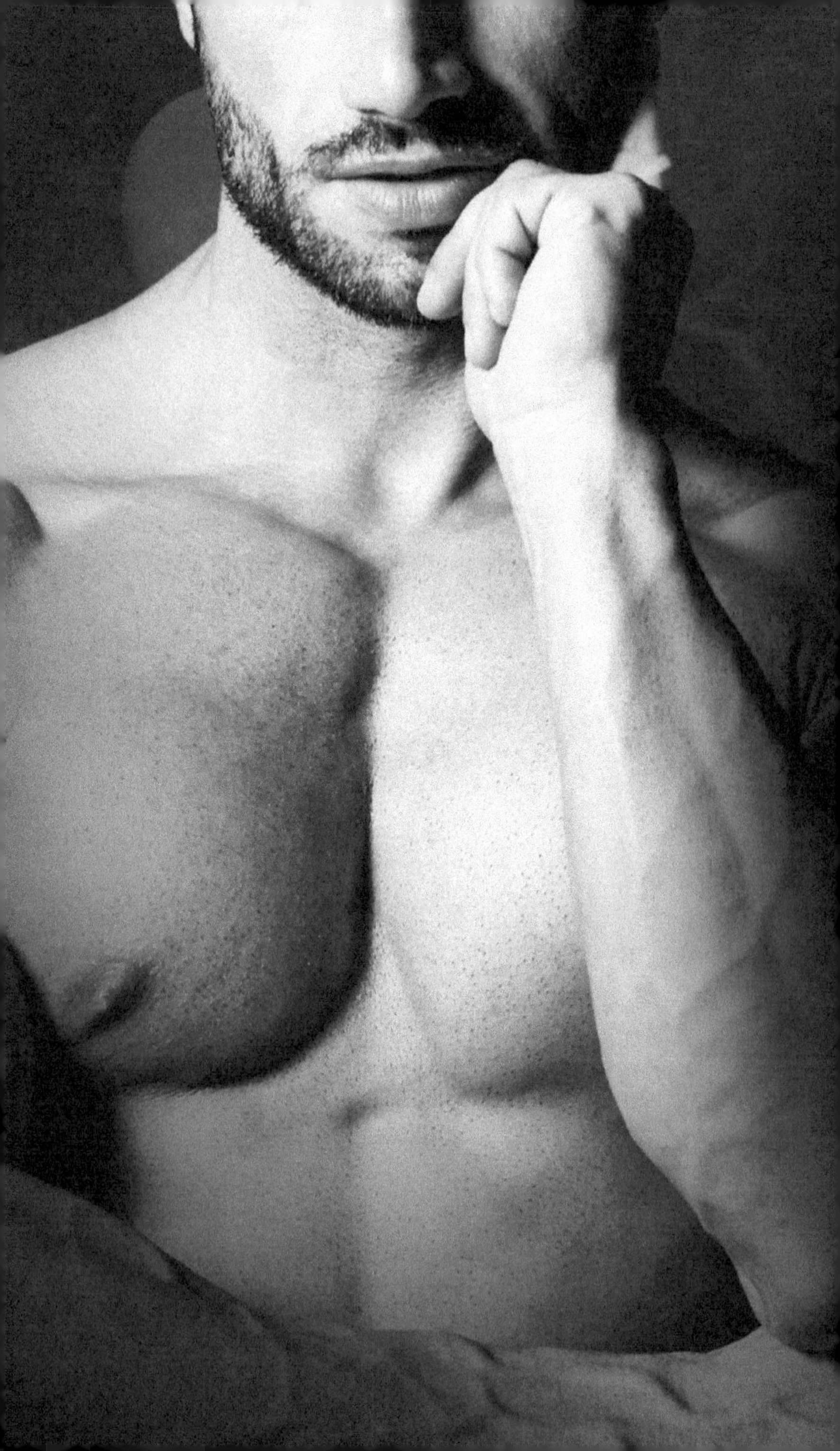

CHAPTER 4
SULLIVAN

I'm still trying to process what just happened as I lean against the cool metal shelves in the back stockroom of Trick or Treat, panting slightly in the aftermath of the kiss that rocked my world off its axis.

"What the fuck?" I mutter to myself, staring at the ceiling. A string of skeleton decorations dangles precariously, seeming to taunt me with their permanent grins. Yeah, I didn't see that coming either.

My brain feels like it's trying to run a hundred different calculations at once, each one more confusing than the last. I'm trying to button my shirt with shaky fingers that don't want to cooperate. Romi is long gone. One second, she was kissing me like there's no tomorrow, and the next, she pulled away and ran out the door like the hounds of hell were on her heels.

By the time I manage to get my clothes somewhat back in order and stumble out into the main part of the bar, it's buzzing with costumed patrons. It feels like every witch, goblin, and what appears to be a disturbingly realistic headless horsewoman is between me and the exit. But there's no sign of Romi.

I'm tempted to tear the bar apart to find her, but the fear of scaring her even more holds me back. I know it's time to take a step back and plan my next move before I really fuck this up and lose my soulmate forever.

I weave through the crowd, peering around every corner, giving my best smile to confused partygoers and slightly annoyed bartenders, but she seems to have vanished into thin air. Frustration grows with every passing minute until I'm left at the bar with nothing but a dwindling sense of hope and a pint of red beer I don't even really want. I mean, not even a real fucking vampire would want to drink this shit.

I linger, trying to convince myself she might reappear, but as I nurse my drink and play through possible scenarios of our second meeting, I'm faced with an unfortunate fact—she's not going to reappear tonight.

When the final call is announced and the bar begins to clear out, I reluctantly head home. I've been bested, chased off like a rookie, my heart still thumping faster than I'd like to admit. But even as I drive back to my home on the family compound, I can't stop replaying the events in the stockroom, wondering when I lost my goddamn heart to the adorable little bar manager.

Once home, I feed my "guard" dog, and I use that term loosely since Angus is scared of his own goddamn shadow. When I bought the house, I decided to go all in and get a dog for company. Everyone said Rottweilers are natural-born protectors, so I decided to get one. Somehow, the little shit I picked out was absent the day the universe handed out protector genes.

I give Angus a little pat on the head and go up to my bedroom for a quick shower. Something tells me I won't be getting any sleep tonight while memories of Romi chase each other through my brain.

My large new home feels too big and too empty tonight. As I wander through the dimly lit halls, muffled echoes of my footsteps underline my solitary state. It's annoying, the way she's lodged herself in my thoughts and my goddamn heart.

When my older brothers found their soulmates, I figured they'd just been stupidly lucky. But now the shoe is on the other foot, and I'm the one with unsolved riddles keeping me awake. Romi's far more enchanting than I'd ever imagined anything, or anyone, could be.

In the morning, or rather, a few hours later, I shuffle into my office at the mansion to attempt to get shit done.

Two hours later, I sit back and rub the base of my neck in frustration. A long stare at my computer's lock screen is the closest to productive work I manage. My mind's still a mess, replaying every single second from last night.

The memories cause my heart to pound while my cock has been hard since the moment I laid eyes on her. Not even coming hard enough for my soul to leave my body made a difference. I'm starting to fucking worry this perpetual erection is damaging something.

Unfortunately, or fortunately, my office is not too far from the house I built after my brothers' respective domestic bliss situations pushed me to stake a claim for myself and escape the love-saturated atmosphere in the mansion. Ironically, I'm now the one knee-deep in restless longing over the little goddess who stole my heart.

I shift uncomfortably in my chair, trying to get comfortable. Around me, framed blueprints of past projects look back at me with quiet judgment. Usually, they motivate the hell out of me, but today, all my spooky creations and haunted ride designs are just glorified paperweights beneath the weight of my brooding.

I almost don't catch the knock at my door. With reluctance, I drag my eyes toward the sound and call out, "Come in," trying my best not to sound like a complete dick.

The door opens, and it's my oldest brother, Sterling, whose entry alongside his goofy grin feels like both a blessing and a curse. He's the last person I want advice from, but sometimes his insightful naivety is what the world needs.

"What's eating you, asshole?" he asks, plopping himself down in a chair across from me, looking like the cat who found out where the cream is kept.

"Who says something's eating me?" I grumble, realizing Romi's tendency to argue has already rubbed off on me.

The dickhead smirks while rubbing his bottom lip. "Now, we're avoiding and deflecting." His armchair psychology is fucking annoying as hell. "Come on, spill. They say confession is good for the soul."

Sighing heavily, I admit defeat. "I met someone." I attempt to keep it nonchalant, but my mental circus makes it nearly impossible to pull off.

His eyebrows perk, his grin turning from goofy to slightly shocked. "As in, the one?" He looks as shellshocked as I feel. "The one," he mutters one more time under his breath.

"Her name is Romi." I trail off, realizing how difficult it is to pin her down with mere adjectives. "She's... incredible. But I somehow managed to fuck everything up and she's run out on me."

"Ah," Sterling remarks, wincing sympathetically. "I think we need to get Adam and Sinclair in here to hear the story."

I shoot him a glare that lacks proper frustration. Adam, his personal assistant, and our middle brother, Sinclair, will chomp at the bit for every little detail they can wrangle from Sterling. "Why? You'll just tell them every goddamn thing later anyway."

"But it's so much better if they hear it from the source."

I huff and raise my middle finger to him. "Fuck you." It's a weak gesture, but it's all I can manage right now.

He pulls his phone out of his pocket, and I'm betting he's messaging my pain and unhappiness to the family group chat before looking back up at me. "You're off your game. Meeting your soulmate does it to the best of us, but don't worry. We've got your back." That's exactly what I'm fucking worried about. "I'd start with calling the bar. See if anyone knows where she might be." I hate it when the fucker comes up with perfectly reasonable solutions I should've thought of myself.

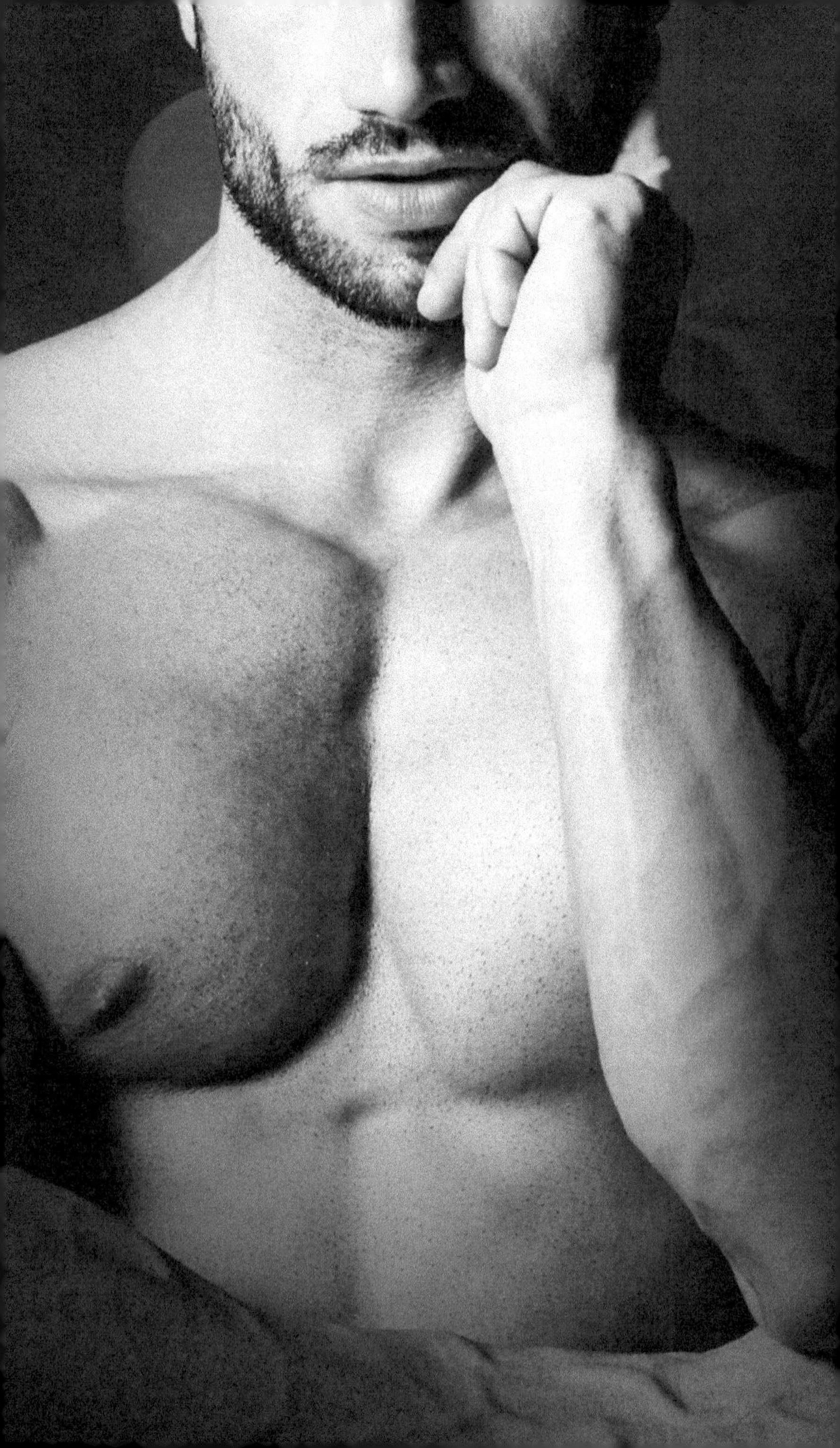

CHAPTER 5
ROMI

After a long sleepless night, I'm sporting dark raccoon eyes and a good case of bedhead. I spent the entire night tossing and turning like a fish out of water, absolutely kicking my own rear end for bolting out on Sullivan like I was being chased by a pack of werewolves.

Sure, my heart was pounding out of my chest, but it wasn't from fear. Well, not the kind of fear you'd find in a haunted theme park, anyway. No, this throb was pure adrenaline mixed with scary emotions caused by the shocking connection I felt with him.

Fast forward through a night devoid of any dreamless sleep, and I'm back at Trick or Treat, sleeves rolled up, and trying to focus on the mundane comfort of restocking the bar.

The bar is still quiet, save for a few early-bird regulars who treat this place like their own personal coffee shop, which is fine as long as they're paying. I'm trying to immerse myself in lining up the bottles of top-shelf spirits exactly three-and-a-half inches from the ledge when suddenly, the hair on the back of my neck stands up like the universe flipped the switch labeled "cosmic chemistry."

I don't even need to turn around to know Sullivan just walked through the door. My pulse kicks up, ricocheting between excitement and anxiety. Part of me is elated, hoping maybe he's here to sweep me off my weary feet and prove our connection wasn't a fluke. The other part of me? Well, it's scanning for the nearest escape route.

Sullivan Midnight owns the room. Not just because his family basically founded the town, but because he's got this magnetic aura about him. Tall, dark, and handsome in the kind of way that sets my entire system on high alert and causes my lady bits to wake up and sing even after the solo-workout they got last night.

Time to confront what I very stupidly ran away from. Swallowing hard, I paste a resolute, easy-going smile onto my face and prepare to turn around and face him, heart pounding like I've downed five espressos too many.

The late afternoon bar atmosphere feels suddenly warm and crowded, even though there's just a spattering of patrons. I feel a little better when I notice how disheveled he looks. Of course, he somehow still manages to carry the devilish, "I've come to suck your blood," kind of appearance. His dark hair is tousled more than it was last night, and those bright blue eyes scan the room, settling on me with a look that's somewhere between happy to see me and ready to strangle me.

"Good afternoon, or whatever passes for it in our little nocturnal town," I greet, and trying to play it cool, slide the bottle into perfect alignment without dropping it.

"Hello, Romi." His voice, deep with a hint of unspoken things that could consume us both if we're not careful, tugs at something deep inside me. The fact that he says my name like it's some kind of invocation doesn't help my mushy heart or hussy girly parts.

"Hi." I paste a bright smile on my face that's as fake as the Louis Vuitton purse in my locker.

Sullivan slides onto a barstool and stares into my soul. "Got time for a chat?"

I blink, caught between wanting to confess every wild thought that's invaded my sleep and keeping them all tucked away safely on some dusty mental shelf. "I can talk and work at the same time. Let's call it multitasking." I gesture with a bar towel, trying to sound more playful than awkward. "As long as you don't mind talking amidst hangover remedy requests and cocktail prep."

He laughs, a sound rich enough to turn me into a puddle of goo. "I'm up for the challenge. Anyway, I wanted to apologize about last night."

Woah. Not what I expected. "Apologize?" I put my hands on my hips, eyebrows knitting together in genuine confusion. "If anything, I'm the one who should be apologizing for running out on you."

He leans forward, those sapphire eyes capturing mine. "I can see we really need to talk, little treat, and there's no way I'm letting you get away from me a second time." Intense Sullivan is way the heck more dangerous to my heart than the teasing version I met last night. I swallow, not knowing how to handle him like this. He's laying it out, unabashed, holding none of his cards too close to his chest.

Something shifts between us, a silent agreement hanging in the air along with the memory of our last encounter among the stockroom shadows. "I know... but I can't have this conversation at work." I fell in love with this crazy town the first moment I stepped foot in it, and I don't want anything to jeopardize my job or future in Midnight Falls.

Sullivan leans against the bar, his demeanor a mix of roguish and charming, like a hero straight out of a romance book—only I never imagined those dreamy characters making my heart pound faster than a bat in a belfry. The air between us feels charged with something new, something electric, and I decide it's time to stop overthinking everything and jump in with both feet.

"Would you have dinner with me," he starts, his voice cutting through the air surrounding us like warm butter, "so we can discuss things?"

"Like a date?" I don't want any other confusion or misunderstandings between us.

"Yes. The first of many I plan to have with you." I'm lost in those striking blue eyes that brim with a sincerity that sends my heart into a little happy dance.

"And if I say no?" I can't help myself—arguing is in my blood.

"Then I'd have to find a way to change your mind." His words send electricity flowing down my spine as I fight the urge to beg him to try.

"Oh. Then I guess I'll save you the trouble and just say yes." I mean, I wasn't really going to turn him down.

He blinks in surprise and then chuckles. "I was already gearing up with a list of counterpoints for your arguments."

"I do enjoy a good argument," I admit with a shrug.

"And I enjoy arguing with you," he replies with a grin. "See all we have in common?" I want to kiss his soft, warm lips again more than I want my next breath. "So, when's your next night off?"

"Tomorrow," I reply, trying to sound casual, but there's a thrill threading through my voice that I can't quite hide. Why pretend though? He seems to like my real self more than any masked version I might come up with, anyway.

"Perfect." He grins, bestowing on me that dazzling, slightly mischievous grin that could probably melt glaciers faster than climate change. "How about dinner at my house?"

My brain does a quick, anxious flip. Alone at his house. Swallowing, I throw caution to the wind. "Dinner sounds great," I say, hoping he doesn't notice the flush moving across my face.

"Great!" Sullivan replies, looking genuinely happy and a little relieved at my agreement. "I'll pick you up around seven if that works?"

"I can do seven, but I'll drive myself to your house." My older sister would kick my rear end if I let a guy I just met pick me up. Even if he's a billionaire. I can hear her *safety-first* speech echoing through my mind.

He opens his mouth and closes it before taking a deep breath and agreeing. "If you insist on driving, I'll give you my address." He takes my phone from me and types his address in my notes app.

With our plans set, he leans over the bar to give me a quick, panty-melting kiss before leaving. After he walks out, the air seems to lose some of its spark. But there's an indelible excitement left behind, reminding me that this is good, right? I mean, it's only my freaking heart and soul at risk. No big deal at all.

I return to my bar duties with a new kind of energy, popping caps off bottles and slinging jokes to patrons with ease. But as I'm mentally running through my wardrobe options for tomorrow night, out comes Tony, lumbering from his office with a look of concern visibly written on his face.

"Romi," he leans close so no one else can hear our conversation, "is Sullivan Midnight bothering you?"

Tony's a big bear of a man, and his concern for his staff is unmatched. He might come across as gruff, but he once gave me the day off when my landlady's cat got stuck in a tree, so I've got a soft spot for the guy. His usual scruffy demeanor is earnest, and I know he'd sooner run through a fire than let anyone mess around with his crew.

"Sullivan?" I laugh, wiping the bar for the millionth time, just to keep busy. "Not at all. He came in to invite me to dinner."

"And did you agree?" Tony echoes, one eyebrow raising in a classic, skeptical style that only he can pull off.

"I did." I can't believe I'm discussing my love life with my grumpy ex-mob captain boss. "I'm looking forward to it." I give him the slimmed-down version, leaving out the part where I jumped Sullivan's bones in the back stockroom.

Tony studies me like he's checking to see if I'm spinning tales or genuinely okay. "I'm glad to hear it. I want you to come to me if you have any problems."

"Thank you." I smile up at him, thanking my lucky stars I found such a wonderful boss.

"You're welcome." Tony nods, throwing an exaggerated watchful glance over the assembled patrons.

Tony heads back to his office while I pull myself together, getting ready to deal with God knows what once the bar gets hopping.

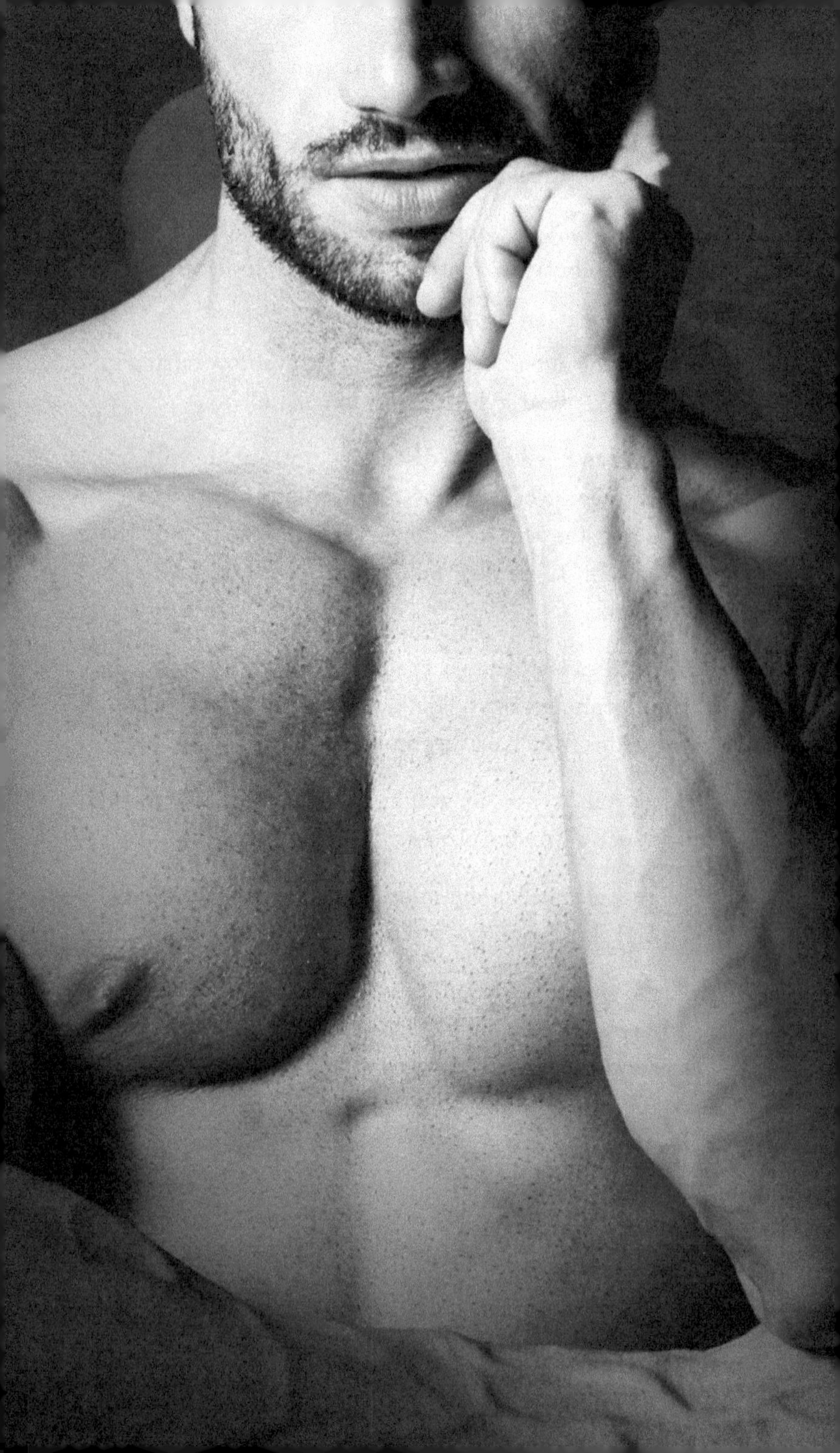

CHAPTER 6
SULLIVAN

I'm in the kitchen, and it's a war zone. Not because I'm bad at cooking—well, not totally—but because I'm trying to do everything at once, and I'm beginning to suspect I might have bitten off more than I can chew. But hey, how hard can it be to boil a few potatoes, toss a salad, and get the steaks ready for the grill for a cozy dinner with Romi? Right?

I've got the apron on complete with a goofy phantom pattern, courtesy of last year's Christmas, and the playlist is a tangle of classic rock and cheesy love songs.

Angus is lying with his back against the sliding glass door, letting the late afternoon sun warm him like he doesn't have a care in the world. Which, for the spoiled rotten Rottweiler, he pretty much doesn't.

I'm about to season the steaks when there's a heavy knock at my front door. It can only be one person who'd hammer like that and not think twice. Sure enough, in strides Sinclair, my dipshit big brother, who also doubles as the town sheriff. Typical. The man's practically an institution around here, mostly because he makes interrogations feel like pleasant chats over coffee and doughnuts.

"If it isn't the elusive Bachelor of Midnight Falls!" he calls as he crosses into my kitchen, eyes roaming over the culinary chaos I've unleashed. "Why haven't you been picking up your phone? Did you already manage to fuck everything up?"

I groan inwardly, realizing the family grapevine somehow moves info faster than an illegal drag race. "Let me guess who told you about Romi." I roll my eyes at the asshole. "Sterling."

"Of course." He laughs, plopping himself onto a barstool in the corner. Angus ambles over for a little pat from my asshole brother before heading back to his favorite spot in the house. "Our brother can't keep a secret to save his life except for where he hides his secret stash of candy."

The timer pings, reminding me the potatoes need to be removed from the heat, and I mutter something about family privacy being a long-lost art as I grab an oven mitt. "Great, are you here to help or to criticize?"

"Depends," Sinclair says with a grin, eyeing the mess I've made of my kitchen. "I'll help you get everything prepped, but I'm not touching that pile of dishes." He gestures at the stack of dishes filling the double sink and overflowing onto the marble countertop.

"Whatever." I ignore the fucker and turn back to the steak and veggies I'm about to marinate. "I don't have time to deal with your stupidity today."

But Sinclair just chuckles, rising to inspect the scene I call organized chaos. "From the looks of this kitchen, I believe you."

I glare at him, pointing a spatula in his direction. "You're not helping. Help or get the fuck out."

He holds his hands up in mock surrender, eyes sparkling with mischief. "Alright, alright." He rolls up his sleeves and opens my dishwasher. "If you ever tell my wife I know how to do this, I'll kill you in your sleep," he grumbles and gets started loading the various cooking utensils in the dishwasher. "And I'll get away with it. Angus would prefer to live with us anyway."

"Only because you give him all the treats." I roll my eyes and smile despite myself. "Don't worry, it'll be our little secret."

"That means you don't tell Sterling or Adam," Sinclair adds, and I nod my head in agreement. He might be a jerk, but he isn't a dumb jerk. "You know the Midnight family network runs faster than the speed of light?" He's not wrong and I'm completely desperate.

"Whatever," I mutter, ready to agree to anything to get some help. The kitchen begins to look less like a battlefield after Sinclair and I engage in a coordinated cleanup effort. It's surprising what two brothers can accomplish when they pause their banter and put their heads together. We work side by side, wiping down surfaces, tidying up the stray pots and pans, and ensuring no trace of spud splatter or seasoning chaos is left behind.

Sinclair is washing the last of the pans when he asks, "What did you get for dessert?"

"Fucking hell." I almost smack my goddamn forehead at the fucking oversight. My mind races. In the flurry of prepping, I'd completely overlooked a final note for the meal. "I didn't even think about dessert," I admit, drumming my fingers on the countertop.

"No worries." He shakes his head, adding, "Big brother will take care of everything." Sinclair sighs like a disappointed parent. "I'll swing by the bakery and grab something while you finish straightening up the house."

With a decisive nod and a parting jibe about 'powering down the kitchen from DEFCON 1,' Sinclair heads out the door.

The moment he's gone, I survey the area, plotting my next move while my dog snores annoyingly across the room.

Time slips by faster than I anticipate, each moment filled with dusting, adjusting, and picking apart thoughts of how tonight might unfold.

I'm pacing the floor when the front door swings open and Sinclair struts in, sweet victory radiating from the bakery box he holds aloft.

"Behold! The pièce de résistance." He places the box carefully on the counter. "It's some kind of raspberry dark chocolate torte," he announces. "I bought one to bring home to Amelia." He wiggles his eyebrows. "I'm hoping she'll show her appreciation later tonight."

I gag dramatically. "I don't need to hear all the specifics."

"I don't care. I'm taking Angus with me." He chuckles and heads for the door with my dog on his heels. "I do want the specifics, so I'll bring your dog back tomorrow and get all the details."

"Yes, Dad," I call to him as he leaves with my traitorous canine following happily behind him.

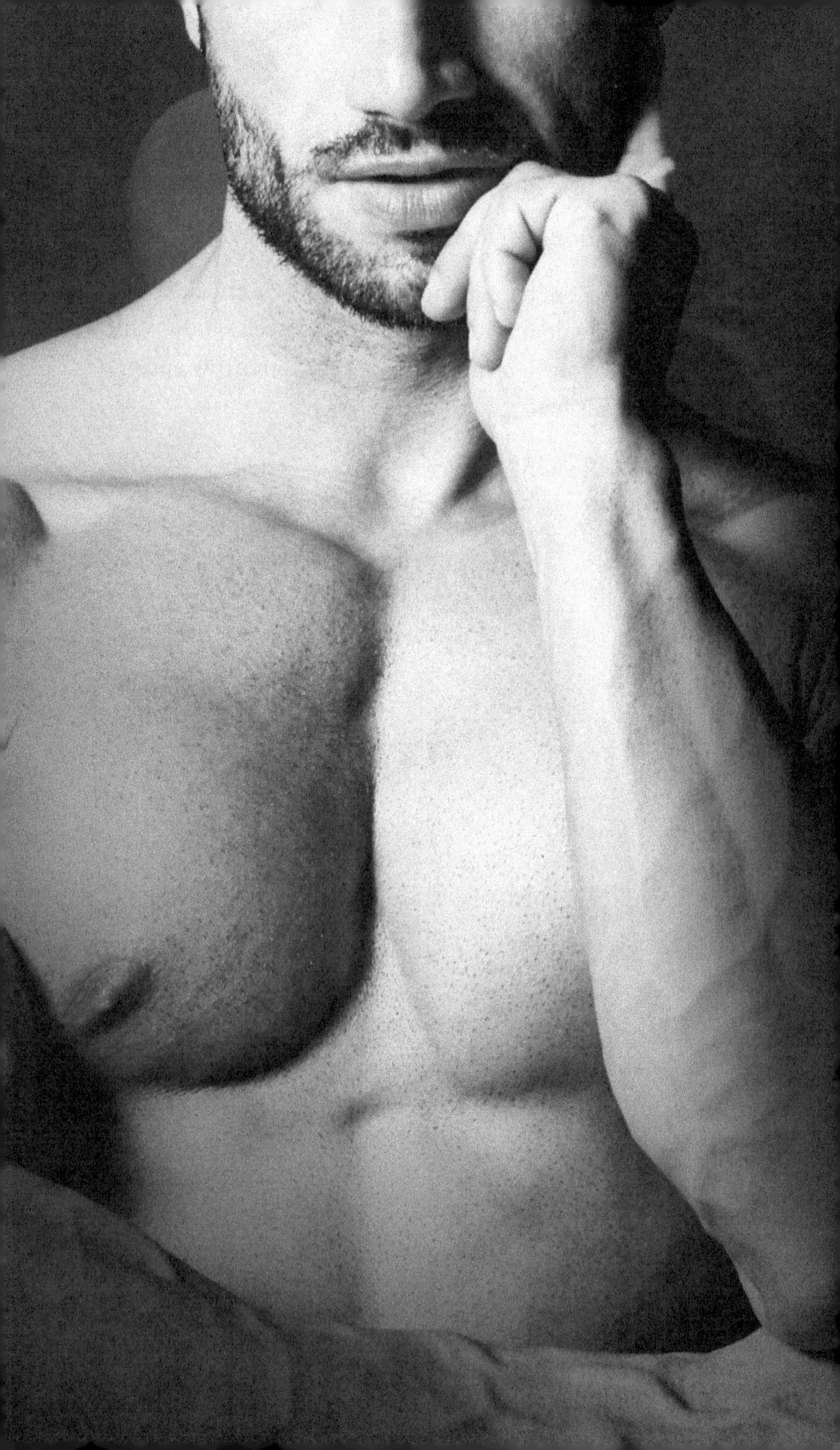

CHAPTER 7
SULLIVAN

The moment I hear the sound of a car pulling up in the driveway, my heart does this odd little flip. My nerves are bouncing up and down like a kid on a sugar high. Before I even realize it, I'm sprinting out the front door, eager to see her, to open the door like some starstruck gentleman from an old movie.

And there she is. Romi. She steps out of the car, and I swear everything else blurs away. She looks so effortlessly gorgeous that I momentarily forget the entire English language. Her hair catches the golden rays of the sunset, and her smile—man, that smile could light up a room full of zombies and make them forget they ever had an appetite for brains.

"Hey, sweetheart," I say, trying to keep my voice casual while grinning like a complete fool.

"Hi," she responds softly, with a spark in her eyes that makes me want to pull her into my arms immediately.

Unable to resist, I do just that. I gather her against me, feeling the warmth of her body as electric chemistry swirls around us. I tilt her chin gently and cover her lips with mine.

Time unravels, and it's just the two of us in this perfect slice of eternity. Her lips are soft and inviting, and I nibble a little on her juicy bottom lip before sliding my tongue into her mouth.

Her curves melt against me, and I groan as my cock turns rock-hard from the feel of her soft body pressing against mine. My hands slide slowly down her back to cup her luscious ass. I lose track of time and place, losing myself in her perfect embrace.

Finally, lack of oxygen causes us to come up for air, and I chuckle a bit once I'm able to catch my breath. "It's a good thing I don't have neighbors," I pant. "Otherwise, we might have given them quite a show."

She laughs, her eyes sparkling with mischief. "Very lucky," she breathes out and reaches up to wipe her lipstick from the corner of my mouth. "This color doesn't work for you," she teases.

"I'll keep that in mind," I joke back, offering her my arm as I lead her inside, feeling the flutter of excitement for what's coming.

As we step into the dining room, I'm suddenly grateful for all the time and effort Sinclair wisely nudged me to invest. The candles flicker on the table, casting a warm, intimate glow that complements the rich aroma of spices.

"Holy cow..." Romi trails off, looking around, clearly impressed. "Your home is stunning."

"I'm glad you like it." I gesture for her to follow me into the kitchen. "Have a seat and I'll get you a glass of wine."

"Thank you." She sits on one of the barstools and watches as I grab two glasses and a bottle of wine. I pour us each a glass and hand hers to her.

"How was your day off?" I ask as I sip the wine Sinclair recommended.

"It was great, but it flew by." She watches as I reach into the refrigerator for the marinated steaks and fresh vegetables.

"Days off seem to do that," I mutter, grabbing everything I'll need to grill our steaks. "I'm going to start the grill. It's the perfect fall evening if you want to come out with me."

She follows me out onto the back patio and watches while I arrange the steak and vegetables on the hot grill.

She laughs, and even the sound is music to my ears. "Wow, your backyard is gorgeous, too."

"Thank you. I love to hang out back here to decompress. Everyone thinks my job is all fun and games, but it's actually stressful as hell," I admit, something I've never told my brothers.

"I can see that." I see the empathy shining in her blue eyes and realize she really does get it. "It must be so stressful to know people could be injured if you mess things up."

Fuck. It's like she goddamn read my mind. If she didn't already own my heart, she would've stolen it at that exact moment. I set an alarm on my phone so I don't turn our food into charcoal, and then I pull her into my arms and cover her lips with mine.

I lose myself as the taste of her flows through me. As I explore her sweet mouth, I forget about everything except my sweet little sassy treat. When the alarm goes off, I reluctantly step back and lay my forehead against hers. "Fucking hell, you're potent."

"So are you." She helps me bring the grilled steaks and vegetables inside. We talk about nothing important while we plate our food.

We settle into easy conversation over dinner. I tell her about my family—the unofficial Midnight royal family of the area, apparently. "My older brother, Sterling, runs the family corporation, Midnight Enterprises. He's got the business savvy and a slightly frightening ability to calculate profit margins in his sleep. Sinclair, my middle brother, is the town sheriff. I'd say he's the law incarnate, but he's actually just a big softy."

"So, do your brothers still treat you like you're a teenager who needs to be protected?"

"How did you know?" It's like she's back to reading my mind.

"I have an older sister who thinks I'm her responsibility even though I've been taking care of myself for years," she admits, and I realize we have way more in common than I'd originally thought. "Older siblings. You can't live with them and you'd look horrible in an orange jumpsuit if you murder them."

"I couldn't agree more." I laugh and pour us each another glass of wine.

"How did you get into haunted ride design?" Romi asks, her gaze steady and curious over the flickering candlelight.

"I always loved to tinker with stuff. Somehow, that led me to studying Mechanical Engineering. From there, I came home and took the head designer job at Midnight Industries and the rest is history."

"I can tell you love it." She leans close, and I barely resist the urge to pull her into my lap.

"There's something thrilling about sculpting the unknown and tapping into people's deepest fears, all the while ensuring they have the time of their lives. There's an art to it," I continue, "finding that fine line between thrilling and terrifying."

She nods as if she genuinely finds my world fascinating. "I can't wait to see one of your masterpieces."

"You've got a standing invite. I'll take you to Midnight Scares anytime you want," I assure her, pleased with the look of anticipation on her face.

"I can't wait! I freaking love haunted houses." She nearly vibrates with excitement, and I fall even deeper under her spell.

As we share the decadent chocolate torte for dessert, I decide it's time to get to know everything about her. "So, what brought you to Midnight Falls?" I ask, feeling the curiosity simmering in my questions.

"The job at Trick or Treat." She shrugs and takes another bite of the torte. "I needed a change of scenery, and I'd heard a ton of great things about Midnight Falls," she replies with a smile.

"And so you could get away from your overprotective sister?"

"That too." She chuckles. "When Tony offered me the job, I jumped at the chance to move here. It didn't go over well with Yvette, but she got over it." Romi gives me this knowing look, her lips curving into a wry grin. "Until she met my landlord. It took a ton of reassurance to get her to leave town after she met Viola."

"Viola?" Surely, she isn't talking about the crazy old lady who regularly terrorizes the town.

"I rent a small garage apartment at Viola Brinkley's house." She chuckles.

"I can't believe you live with old Mrs. Brinkley, the one and only town legend, notorious for her unusual ways." More than unusual. The elderly woman sits on her porch every day in an old floral nightgown with curlers in her hair and a cigarette hanging from her mouth. On

MIDNIGHT TREAT

Halloween, she gives out candy to the kids and small bottles of bourbon to the adults.

Romi shrugs. "I actually love it. She's a doll and her pet iguana, Herman, hangs out in the window surveying his domain."

"Ah, Midnight Falls' very own eccentric grandma," I muse. "You know she's convinced aliens landed in her garden last summer?"

"She might have told me that once or twice," Romi admits, laughing again. There's something infectious about the way her laughter fills the room, chasing away any shadows.

I lean back, marveling at how this evening is turning out even better than I dared to hope. It's not just the chemistry between us, which feels undeniable, or how easy our conversation flows. It's Romi herself. The way she seems to fit naturally amidst the folds of my life like she's been a part of it forever.

"You're fucking perfect," I tell her, sincerity threading through my words. "I'm glad you decided not to have me thrown out of Trick or Treat the night we met."

She meets my eyes, her gaze steady and warm. "It was touch and go for a few minutes," she teases. "But you grew on me—kinda like a fungus. I just couldn't resist you."

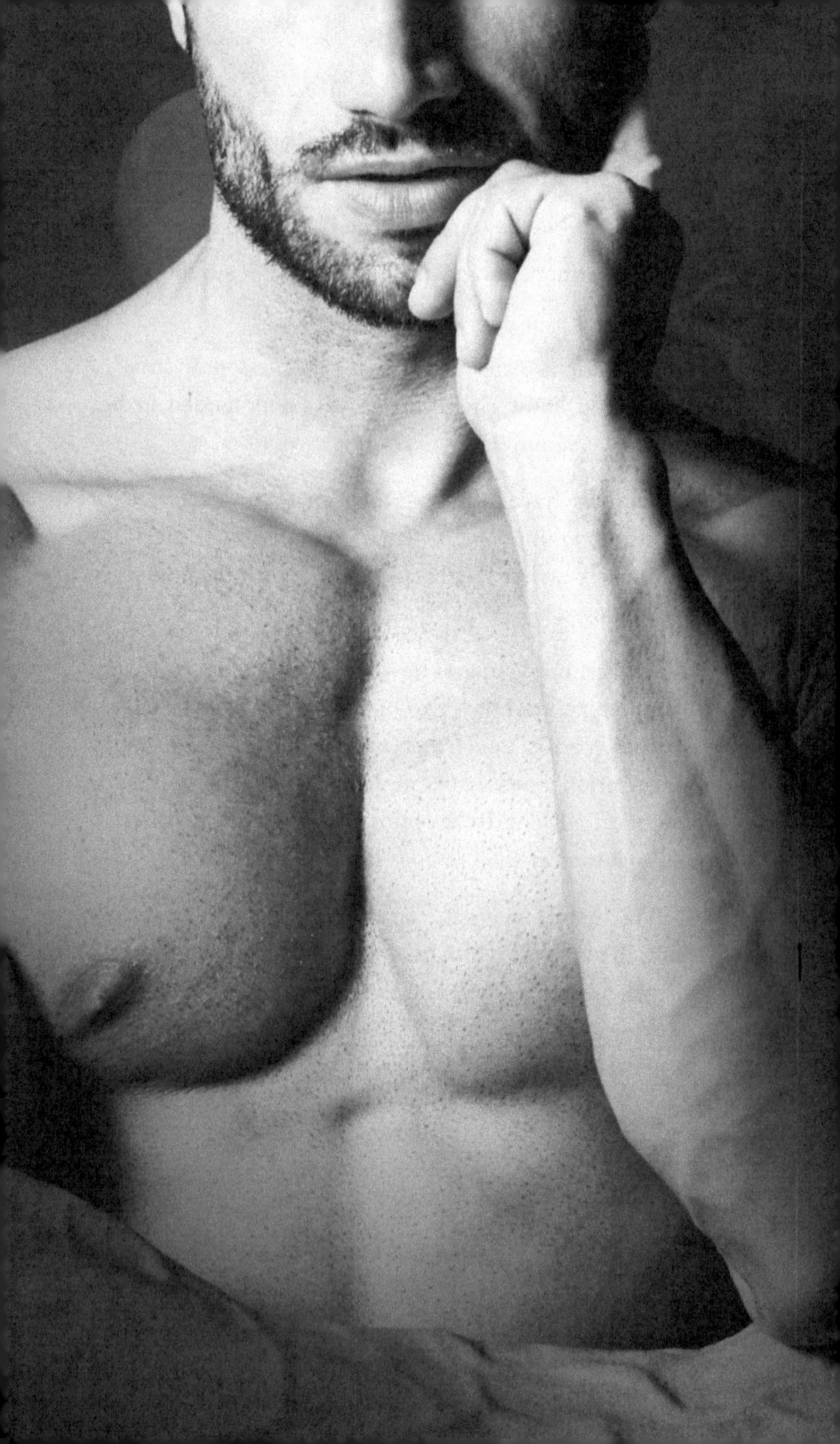

CHAPTER 8
ROMI

That's a freaking understatement. I've spent too long being careful, cautious, thinking ahead, and planning every leap.

I tell myself just to go for it before I lose my nerve.

Leaning in, I kiss him, a soft brush of lips that's not just a test of water, but a full-blown swan dive.

Surprise flickers in his eyes before he wraps his arms around me, pulling me into an embrace that causes my heart to nearly pound out of my chest.

"I hope you don't mind if I take things into my own hands," I mutter as I slide my hand between our bodies. A massive shudder runs through his body as I give his rock-hard cock a little squeeze.

"Do you have any idea what you're doing to me?" he growls and leans over to nibble on the side of my neck.

"I'm trying to make a move on you." I unzip his pants and slide my hand inside. "Am I doing it right?"

"You couldn't do it any better." He kisses me and slides his tongue into my mouth. While our tongues tangle, I wrap my hand around his hardness and give it a little squeeze. When he lifts me against his hard chest, I give a little squeak and curl my arms around his neck to hold on tight as he carries me through his mansion to his bedroom.

He tosses me onto his silk-covered bed and I land in the center, bouncing a few times. He steps back and drags his shirt over his head and tosses it aside, so I decide to follow his lead and remove my shirt. His eyes roam over my curves, heating me up from the inside out.

Wow, I think as I stare at his muscular chest and a set of perfect washboard abs. Biting my bottom lip, I watch as he makes quick work of his shoes and pants. When he prowls toward me, I stare at his massive cock bouncing up against his flat stomach, and a little spark of fear cuts through me. Actually seeing it up close makes me wonder how in the world my virgin lady bits are going to handle all that... maleness.

"I'm not sure this is going to work." I point back and forth between his large erection and my unused girly parts.

"Don't worry, little treat, we'll make this work perfectly," he groans and prowls toward me. I bite my bottom lip and watch as he quickly pulls my yoga pants and underwear down my legs.

"I haven't ever done this before." I spell it out so there are no misunderstandings between us.

"That's good because I can't stomach the thought of another man touching your gorgeous little body."

"There's that caveman attitude I know and love," I grumble lightheartedly without thinking about what I'm saying.

"Get used to it." He wraps his hands around my legs and pulls me to the edge of the bed. His navy-blue eyes hold mine captive while he drops to his knees and runs his hands up my spread thighs. "I love you, little treat." I barely hear his whispered declaration. "I'm about to show you just how much."

"Please touch me," I beg, not sure how to respond so I let my body take over.

My eyes cross when he leans down and places soft kisses along the sensitive skin on the inside of my thigh. He gives a little nibble, distracting me before swiping his tongue straight up my wet center, completely blowing my mind.

He devours my pussy, causing me to lose track of time. When he presses on my clit, pleasure flows through my soul as I go off like a firecracker. I ride out the orgasm while he lightly licks my wet opening.

"Holy cow," I manage to mumble as he slides his finger inside my wet center. He slowly slides a second finger in next to it and scissors them apart, rubbing a very sensitive spot deep inside me.

"My cock is dying to get inside you," he growls.

"Then hurry up." My impatience shows, but he ignores my plea and continues driving me wild with his fingers.

I'm ready to sing halleluiah when he finally drags me to the top of the bed and crawls over me.

He runs his nose along my collarbone, sending goosebumps skittering across my over-sensitized skin. When he rolls my nipple between his thumb and forefinger, I gasp his name and beg him to hurry up.

He finally heeds my pleas and lines his erection up with my wet center. I hold my breath and dig my nails into his shoulders as he pushes deep with one thrust. The bite of the burning stretch only lasts a few seconds. Pretty soon, pleasure flows through me, and I start lifting my hips up to meet his thrusts.

He kisses me and I forget everything except how Sullivan makes me feel. When he presses his thumb in small circles around my clit, the little sparks of pleasure grow into a low burning deep in my core.

He slides his arm under my left leg and lifts it above his shoulder, allowing him to slide a little deeper with each thrust.

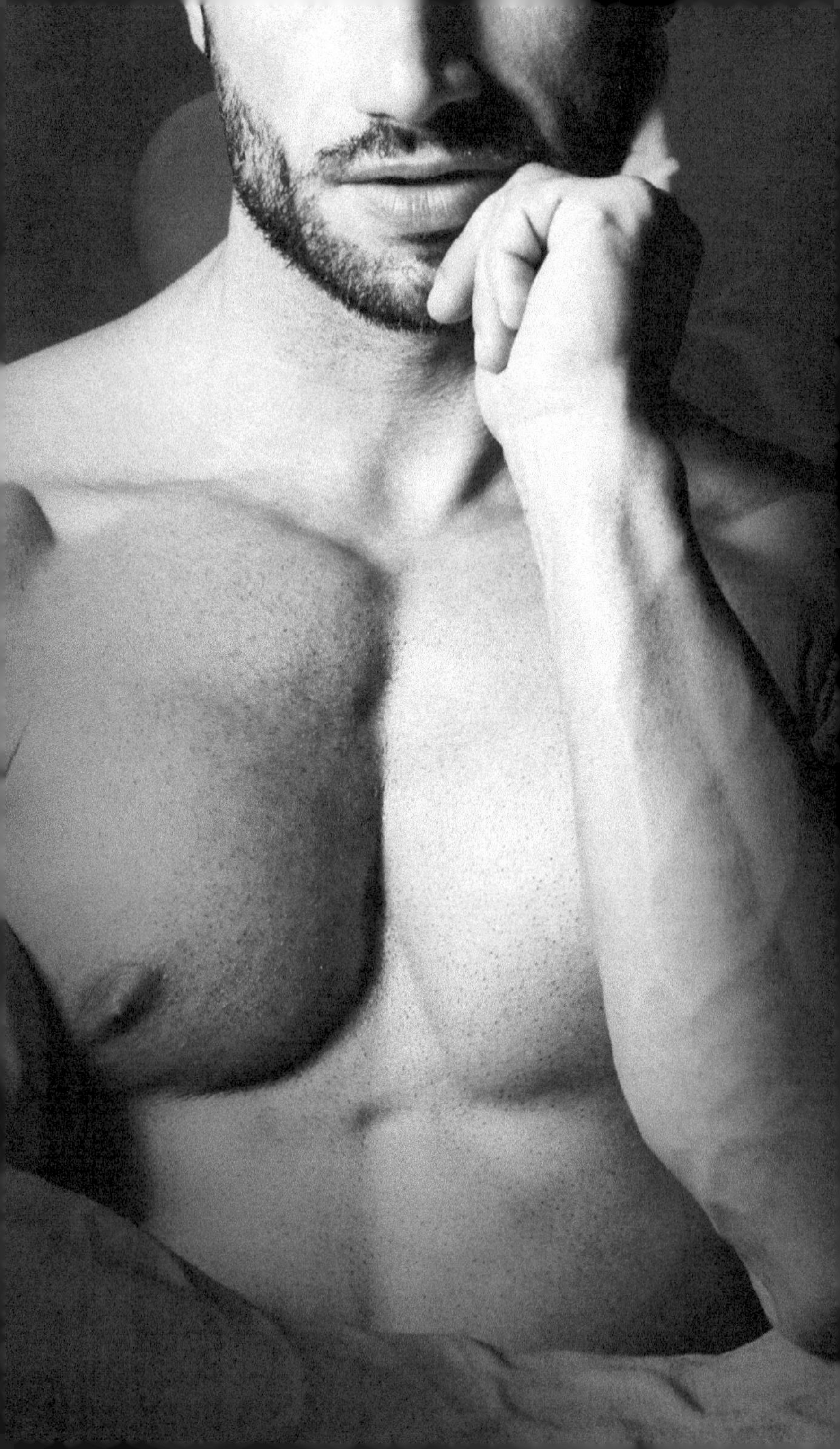

CHAPTER 9
SULLIVAN

She's fucking perfect. Every time I thrust, she whimpers, begging for more, and I can't resist her pleas.

"You're fucking perfect." I lay my forehead against hers as my hips rock from side to side, driving us both closer to orgasm.

I lean over and close my lips around her nipple while driving into her.

Her goddam perfect body is a work of art created just for me, and I fucking love every single inch of it.

She chants my name as I bite down gently on her nipple. Her silky walls ripple around my cock and I barely resist the urge to come.

"Ride me." I spin onto my back and drag her curvy body up over me. Her thighs straddle mine as I hold on to her waist. I use my hold to lift her up and down, showing her how to move.

She throws her hair over her shoulder and leans over to kiss me. Each time she slides down, her inner muscles squeeze the fuck out of my cock, and I know I'm not going to last long.

"Come with me," I order her and lift my hips while rubbing my thumb across her clit, sending her over the edge.

I roar her name and come with her, making sure to spray my cum deep inside her little pussy, hoping my swimmers do their job. Her limp body falls across my chest, and I drag her tousled hair away from her beautiful face and lean up to place a soft kiss on her temple. "I love you, little treat," I repeat, wondering if she even heard me earlier.

"I love you, too, caveman." And just like that—my world shifts on its axis and everything settles into a perfect rhythm.

Waking up with Romi curled up in my arms feels like waking up in the middle of a pretty damn near perfect dream. The even rise and fall of her breathing tells me she's still sound asleep.

Her tousled hair tickles my chin as I shift a little, trying not to disturb her. But fuck, it's impossible not to kiss her. I place a soft kiss on her forehead, intending to sneak out of bed without disturbing her.

The quiet, contented sound coming from her sweet lips goes straight to my heart and wakes up my goddamn cock. Her eyes flutter open slowly and she smiles up at me.

"Morning." I run my nose across the side of her cheek.

She blinks a few times and stretches languidly. "Morning," she replies, voice still thick with sleep.

"What time is it?" she asks, yawning and glancing toward the curtain-covered window.

"Early enough that we can be lazy for a bit," I tell her, my arms tightening around her, reluctant to let go just yet.

"What did you have in mind?" Her tone is playful, eyebrows raised in mock suspicion.

I feign deep thought for a moment, grinning wickedly. "A shower sounds like a good idea."

Before she can object or even fully awaken, I sweep her up in my arms. "Sullivan!" she protests, though she's laughing, too, her arms looping instinctively around my neck. She feels like she was made to be in my arms, one more thing I didn't know I needed before now.

"Get used to it, little treat. I plan to carry your gorgeous ass around all the time from now on."

"That might make both of us working a little difficult," she teases, her voice tinged with amusement and traces of happy surrender.

"We'll figure something out," I tease back.

Setting her down, I take a moment to flick on the bathroom lights before turning turn the water on.

We're dressing when my phone rings. I see Sinclair's ugly mug flash across the screen and sigh. "I have to answer this," I tell her. "My brother is dog-sitting for me and I need to make sure Angus is okay."

"Of course." She smiles and sits back on the bed to pull on her shoes while I answer the call.

"What do you want?" He's interrupting my time with Romi, and I'm not in the mood to deal with his bullshit.

"To let you know I'm about to leave my house to return your menace before he does permanent damage to my goddamn house," Sinclair growls and dives headfirst into a full-blown diatribe about how Angus apparently forgot all the virtues of domesticated life and embraced his inner scoundrel last night. "If I didn't know better," Sinclair grumbles, voice crackling over the line with weary exasperation, "I'd swear Angus is part raccoon. The way he got into the trash can overnight, you'd think he was single-pawedly preparing for a post-apocalyptic food shortage."

I can't stifle my laughter as I imagine Sinclair, my usually unflappable, all-business older brother and town sheriff, being given the runaround by a merry whirlwind of fur and slobber. "You should've given him his late-night snack, and then he wouldn't have had to go searching for food."

"Funny. Real funny, dickhead," Sinclair growls. "See if I help you clean your fucking kitchen next time."

I hear the sound of conversation in the background and realize my brother's frustration led him to blurt out his little secret to his wife. I almost feel sorry for him. Almost.

"Fucker. You're going to come over and help me clean up the mess your menace created," Sinclair insists before hanging up on me.

I drop the phone down on the bedside table and turn to Romi. "Evidently, my dog caused a little trouble at my brother's house, so Sinclair is bringing Angus home right now."

Her expressive eyes widen. "Do you want me to stay up here until he's gone?"

"Fuck no." I take her soft hand in mine. "I fucking love you. I want everyone to know you're mine. I want to hang the bloodstained sheets from the window to tell every goddamn man in town you belong to me."

"It's time to calm down that freaking caveman attitude, Mr. Midnight." She laughs. "I love you, too, but I'd prefer not to have the entire town talking about the loss of my virginity."

A LITTLE WHILE LATER, I HEAR SINCLAIR'S SUV PULLING INTO the driveway, and before long, there's a robust knock on the front door.

Opening the door, I find Sinclair standing on the front porch with a look that's somewhere between stern sheriff and exhausted brother. He holds out Angus's leash to me. "Here's your tornado disguised as man's best friend." I glance down at my dog and find his ears are down in a pathetic attempt to look innocent. Boy, does he know the drill.

"Thanks," I tell my brother as he steps inside. Angus instantly bounds toward me and nuzzles my hand with an earnestness that reminds me of a repentant criminal finally coming clean. "He seems to be apologetic."

"Apologetic, my ass," Sinclair huffs. "That menace is…" Whatever he was about to say about my poor pooch is cut off when Romi steps into the foyer looking radiant and slightly amused.

"Romi, this is Sinclair, the lawman of Midnight Falls and my disaster-management brother." I wave a hand between them, knowing that a handshake and forced pleasantries are inevitable. But damn if there isn't a little flicker of something proprietary glinting inside me when Sinclair extends his hand to hers. Some primal, caveman-like part of me growls, "*Mine*."

"Nice to meet you, Romi," Sinclair says, shooting me a brotherly wink as he releases her hand, letting me know he's got no intentions beyond being charming and relaxed, but still raising my hackles just a bit.

"You too," Romi responds with a grin and steps back over to stand next to me.

While this exchange takes place, Angus sits obediently at Romi's feet, staring up with those soul-penetrating brown eyes. It's like he's trying to communicate telepathically that she's his new favorite human and she should please never leave again.

"Aww, who's this handsome fella?" Romi bends down, giving Angus' ears a rub that would have any dog instantly devoted. If Angus could speak, I'm sure he'd be composing love sonnets.

"This is Angus," I reply, arms crossed and playfully indignant. "The family rogue. Sinclair just brought him back from one of his infamous trash-diving escapades."

Romi laughs, and it's a sound that always manages to brighten rooms. "Angus, you and I will need to have a chat about your desire to dumpster dive."

Sinclair watches the scene, clearly amused. "Looks like Romi's won him over already. Not that it surprises me." He gives me a knowing look, and I barely resist the urge to roll my eyes at him. "I hate to run off, but I have to get home and help clean up the disaster your menace made."

As the door closes behind him, I turn to see Romi's transition into total puppy love. Angus is right there with her as if they've always been a package deal, his tail wagging at the speed of happiness. "Now, don't go trying to steal my girl," I tell my spoiled fucking rotten canine.

"Too late." Romi glances up at me and smirks. "He's too hard to resist." She scratches under his chin, and Angus, traitor that he is, settles in like he's found his forever human. "I think he's going to be my cuddle bug."

Angus basks in the attention, and I can hardly blame him as I watch the genuine connection forming between them.

"We should go for a walk in the park," I suggest, seizing the chance to let go of daily chores mislabeled as exercise. "If we get him enough exercise, he'll be too tired to cause any trouble later."

"It sounds like a plan to me." She doesn't hesitate. After finding his walking harness, we head out to my truck.

"I warn you, he's a menace in the park," I mention playfully as we drive toward town with Angus sitting up front between us.

"I can't see this sweetie ever being a menace," Romi counters. Fucking hell. She's already fallen for the canine's charms.

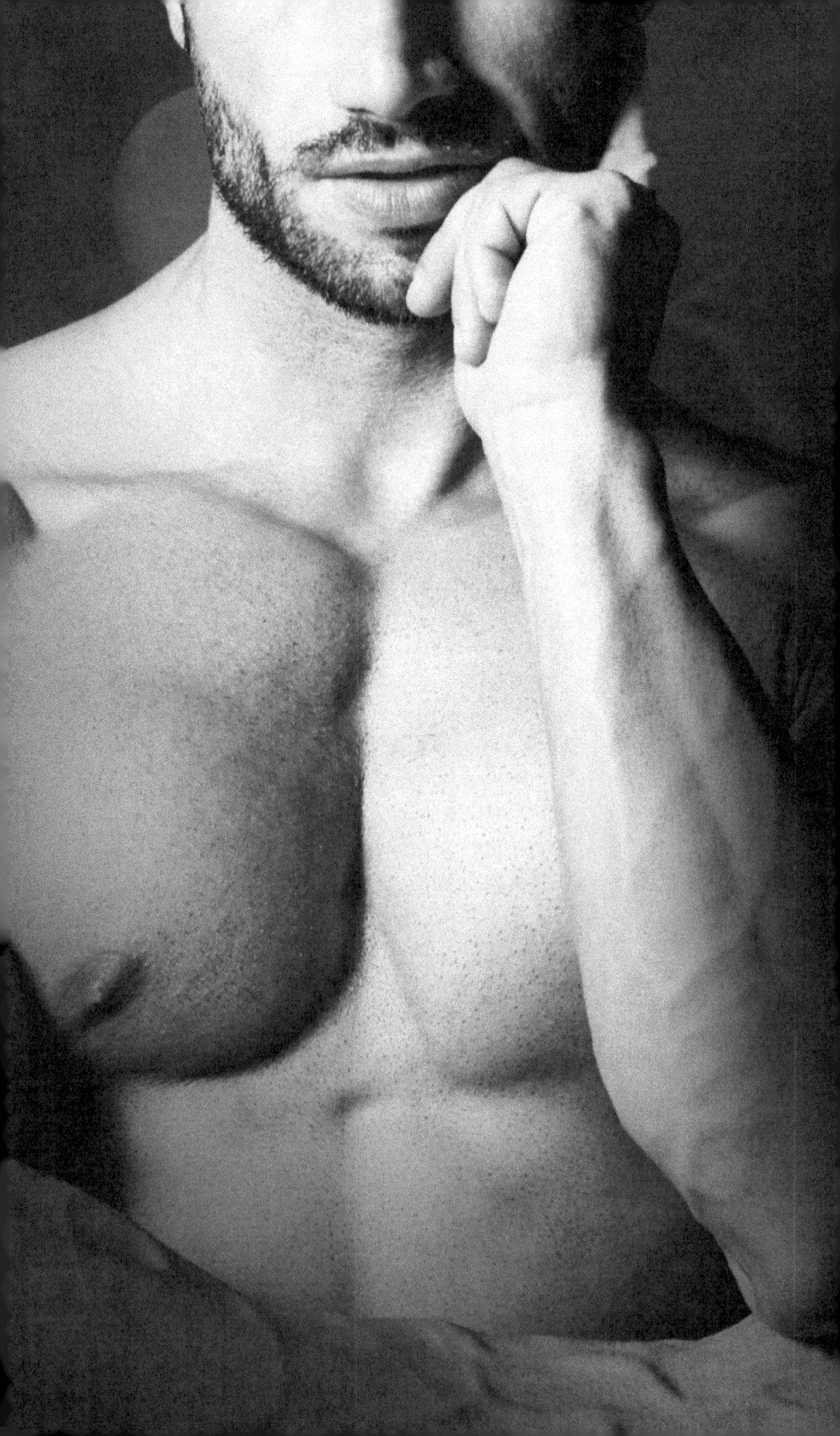

CHAPTER 10
ROMI

The afternoon sun casts a warm, honey-like glow over everything as Sullivan drives me back to my apartment. The memory of our morning in the park with Angus keeps a goofy grin plastered on my face.

As we pull into the driveway, I glimpse the ever-vigilant Ms. Viola positioned on her front porch, a steadfast queen overseeing her suburban kingdom. Her hair is in curlers, adding a touch of 1950s glam to her otherwise mismatched outfit of leisure wear, completed by a long, lazy cigarette drooping precariously from one corner of her mouth. And there's Herman, the old iguana, basking on the banister, looking as if he might issue a decree at any moment about who does or doesn't belong in his sunlit spot.

Sullivan puts the truck in park and turns to me. "Here we are," he announces as though we've trekked through distant lands instead of just down the road. There's a moment where neither of us particularly wants to move.

"I really had a great time today." I lean over and place a soft kiss on his lips. "And last night."

"Me too." Sullivan wraps his hand around the back of my head and draws me closer.

His warms lips close over mine and my mind shuts down. As he devours my mouth, I forget all about my new canine friend in the back seat and my landlady sitting on the front porch.

When he pulls back, I blink several times, trying to clear the fog from my mushy brain. He tells me, "I'll see you later on, little treat."

"I have to work tonight," I blurt out the first thing that comes to mind. God, he just has to look at me to turn me into a bubbling airhead. What in the world is happening to me? Oh yeah. Sullivan stole my heart and blew my mind at the same time.

"I know. I'll be there tonight to make sure no asshole decides to take his life into his own hands by touching my girl." His territorial words should raise my hackles, but they do the opposite.

"Okay." I smile at him and give Angus one more scratch under the chin. Sullivan comes around the side of the truck and opens the door for me. Angus grumbles in the backseat about being left in the truck, but Sullivan ignores his disgruntled canine and takes my hand in his.

As we walk up the sidewalk, he gives my hand a reassuring squeeze. "Good afternoon, Ms. Viola."

"Mr. Midnight." I'm not sure how that cigarette stays balanced on her bottom lip while she talks. "You kept my tenant out all night last night," she states, and I groan to myself.

"Yes, ma'am, I did." Sullivan wraps his arm around my shoulders. "And I'm planning to keep her out a lot more in the future."

"Just make sure you put a ring on her finger before you put a bun her the oven." I feel my face heat from her words, and I wonder if the universe would do me a solid and have the ground open up and swallow me on the spot.

"I'm planning on doing that, too," Sullivan reassures her.

"Good." She seems satisfied with his responses, and Herman turns his head, slowly blinking one beady eye in our direction, a slight nod of sage approval. "Just so you know, Herman approves, and he's got a better judge of character than most folks I know," Ms. Viola adds as a puff of her smoke drifts across the front porch.

"I'm glad to have his approval," Sullivan laughs and leans over the banister to give the lounging reptile prince a little pat on the head. He responds with a flick of his tongue, clearly already over our banal human exchanges.

Ms. Viola chuckles, flicking her cigarette ash casually over the railing before glancing over at me. "Don't waste time when you know a good one. Boys like him don't come knocking every week, darling. Trust me. I've had my fair share of door knocks."

"Don't worry, I don't plan on ever letting him go." I've never been more sure about anything in my life.

"Good." She nods, a slow confirmation that carries wisdom, and then she totally throws me under the bus in front of my caveman. "Go clean yourself up, honey. I don't know what you did with that man, but you smell like dog and sunshine."

"Oh my God," I mumble under my breath as Sullivan laughs.

"I'm going to walk Romi up to her door if you don't mind, Ms. Viola?"

"I wouldn't have it any other way, Mr. Midnight."

Taking that cue, we walk around the back of the house to my apartment. At my door, Sullivan pulls me into his arms and kisses me to within an inch of my life.

When Angus starts barking nonstop from the truck, Sullivan lays his forehead against mine and groans, "I'm going to start buying the cheap treats if he keeps cock blocking me."

"No, you aren't." I laugh and step into my living room before I'm tempted to forget all about his spoiled pooch and my crazy landlady and drag him inside. "I'll see you later, caveman."

"Yes, you will, little treat."

I watch him walk away before shutting the door and leaning against it. Wow.

MIDNIGHT TREAT

It's a typical night at Trick or Treat, the bar hopping with the usual mix of quirky costumed locals and wide-eyed tourists trying to capture the perpetual Halloween magic of Midnight Falls.

I'm in full-on bartender mode, hands flying over the array of bottles, trying to keep up with the various orders.

I can feel him. Sullivan is here, and no matter how fast I whip up Witching Hour cocktails or dodge strong opinions about which villain karaoke round we should feature next, there's an electric current pulsing whenever I meet his gaze, even from across the room.

At the far end of the bar, Sullivan sits nursing his beer. His eyes follow me, a mischievous glint in their blue depths that brightens especially when I glance his way.

Over the clinking of glasses and bubbly chatter, Tony, my intimidating boss, sidles up next to Sullivan. They exchange a few words, their interaction soft enough to stay below the radar of my attentive customers but visible enough to twinge my curiosity to unbearable levels.

What are they talking about? I imagine Sullivan's made some sort of gentlemanly vow or Tony rattled out big-boss warnings torn from mobster movie monologues. My shoulders twitch with the effort not to fill margarita pitchers with shaking hands, the concoction as brightly colored as the glow from the ridiculous pumpkin head lamp anchoring the bar's Halloween theme.

I slide another rolled napkin next to a colorful tower of shots in front of the middle-aged witch who's been overly generous with her tipping all night, subtly peering down the bar to gauge what the heck is happening down there.

When Tony walks away and Sullivan doesn't appear to be overly concerned about my boss, I breathe a sigh of relief.

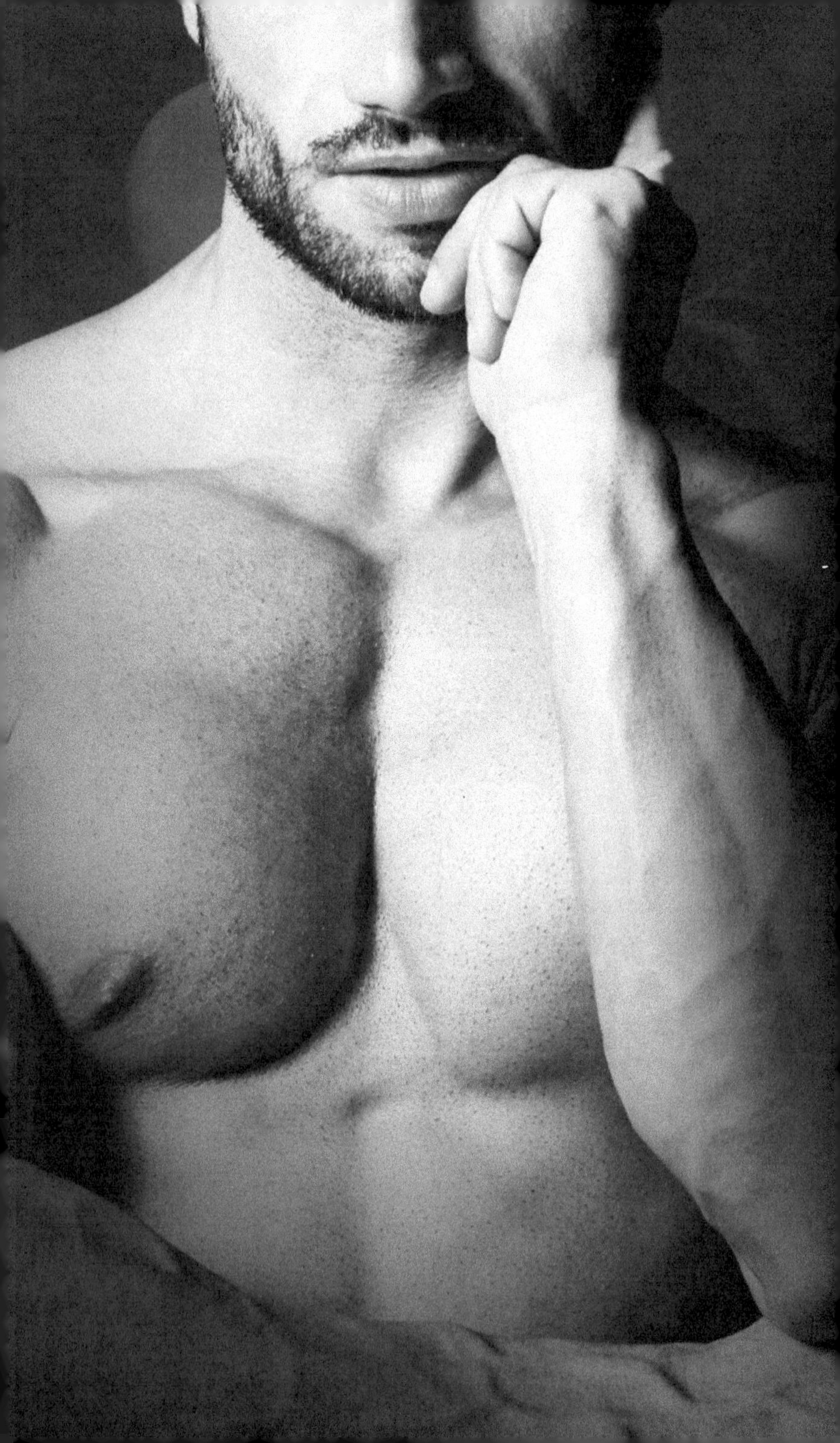

CHAPTER II
SULLIVAN

I COVER HER SOFT LIPS WITH MINE, LETTING HER TASTE FLOW through my soul. "I missed you today," I mumble against her silky lips.

"I was only gone for five hours," she whispers back, knowing I love to spar with her.

"Five hours too many," I groan and slide my tongue around the pulse beating at the base of her silky neck. "My cock is about to rebel if he doesn't get inside you soon." I back her up to the bed while fighting the urge to forget all finesse and fuck her until we both are too tired to breathe. As the backs of her thighs bump against the edge of the bed, she falls and lays back, staring up at me.

"Hurry up." Her impatience matches mine, and she doesn't have to ask me a second time. It only takes me a couple of seconds to tear away my clothes and toss them off somewhere in the corner. "That's more like it." She sits up a little bit and pulls off her concert t-shirt and pink lace demi bra. My cock turns to stone as I watch her perfect tits jiggle around.

"You're so fucking gorgeous," I hiss when she drags her yoga pants down her silky legs and kicks them aside.

Leaning over her, I place my hands on either side of her head and lean over to kiss her pouty lips.

"Touch me." My growl turns into a moan when she slides her soft hand between us and wraps it around my cock. Her delicate touch sends sparks shooting down my spine, and I don't resist when she pushes me onto my back and kisses her way down my chest. I almost come like a teenager when she pauses along the way to nibble on my sensitive skin.

When she finally makes her way all the way down my body, my cock practically sings while waiting for her attention.

I dig my head back into the soft covers and recite multiplication tables in my mind, attempting to hold off my orgasm while she explores my dick. When she runs her tongue up the front of my cock, a shiver runs through my entire body.

"Suck it." I can't wait any longer.

She glances up and stares into my eyes with a raised eyebrow. "Be patient and let me check things out."

She squeaks adorably when I smack her gorgeous ass. "You can check things out later. Right now, I want you to suck my cock between those perfect goddamn lips."

MIDNIGHT TREAT

"If you insist." She winks at me and follows my orders. I dig my heels into the bed as her soft lips part for my cock. When she runs her tongue lightly over the head, I stare at the ceiling, enjoying my little treat's efforts.

As the urge to come becomes insistent, I pull back. "Hey," she grumbles. "Why are you stopping me?"

I lay her back on the bed and lean over to smile at her. "Because I'm not wasting any of my little swimmers until I've knocked your sweet ass up."

"Oh." She blinks up at me as I kiss my way across her collarbone and down her luscious body. When I spread her legs and slide my tongue deep inside her wet pussy, she digs her fingers into the back of my head and tugs me closer.

After running my tongue around her tight opening, I suck her clit between my lips and bite down gently. When I slide a finger into her pussy, her silky walls clamp down around my digit, causing my cock to grow impatient.

I spread her pussy lips wide open and slide my tongue deep while her inner muscles flutter. When I press my finger against her tight little clit, she orgasms, screaming my name.

While the tremors run through her curvy frame, I kiss my way back up her luscious body. I stop along the way to give each of her tits a little attention before lining my cock up with her tight opening.

"Please," she begs as I cover her lips with mine.

"I fucking love you," I pull my mouth away from hers and mutter against her soft lips.

She digs her sharp fingernails into my shoulders. "Show me how much...ahh..."

I press deep with one thrust, cutting off the rest of her sentence. I really intend to take things slowly and enjoy every second of being deep inside her sweet pussy, but my little treat has other ideas.

She wraps her leg around my waist and lifts her hips, forcing my dick deeper. I circle my hips, picking up speed while her intimate muscles strangle the fuck out of my cock. Sweat breaks out on my face, and I lose track of time as I make love to my little treat.

When a climax starts tingling at the base of my spine, I reach between us to press on her tight little clit. My eyes roll back in my head as I come deep in her sweet pussy.

"I love you so goddamn much," I growl against her soft neck when I'm able to catch my breath. "You stole my heart the second you made fun of my name in the Trick or Treat stockroom."

I roll over and pull her close. "I love you, too." She sighs, snuggling into my embrace. I reach over to turn off the light and she whispers, "I hope it's okay for me to spend the night."

"I don't ever plan on letting you spend the night anywhere else again."

At some point during the night, Angus decides he doesn't like sleeping alone and crawls up in bed with us. When I wake up clinging to one side of the bed while Romi clings to the other side, I realize we're going to have to find a way to convince my spoiled pooch to sleep in his fancy bed in front of the fireplace.

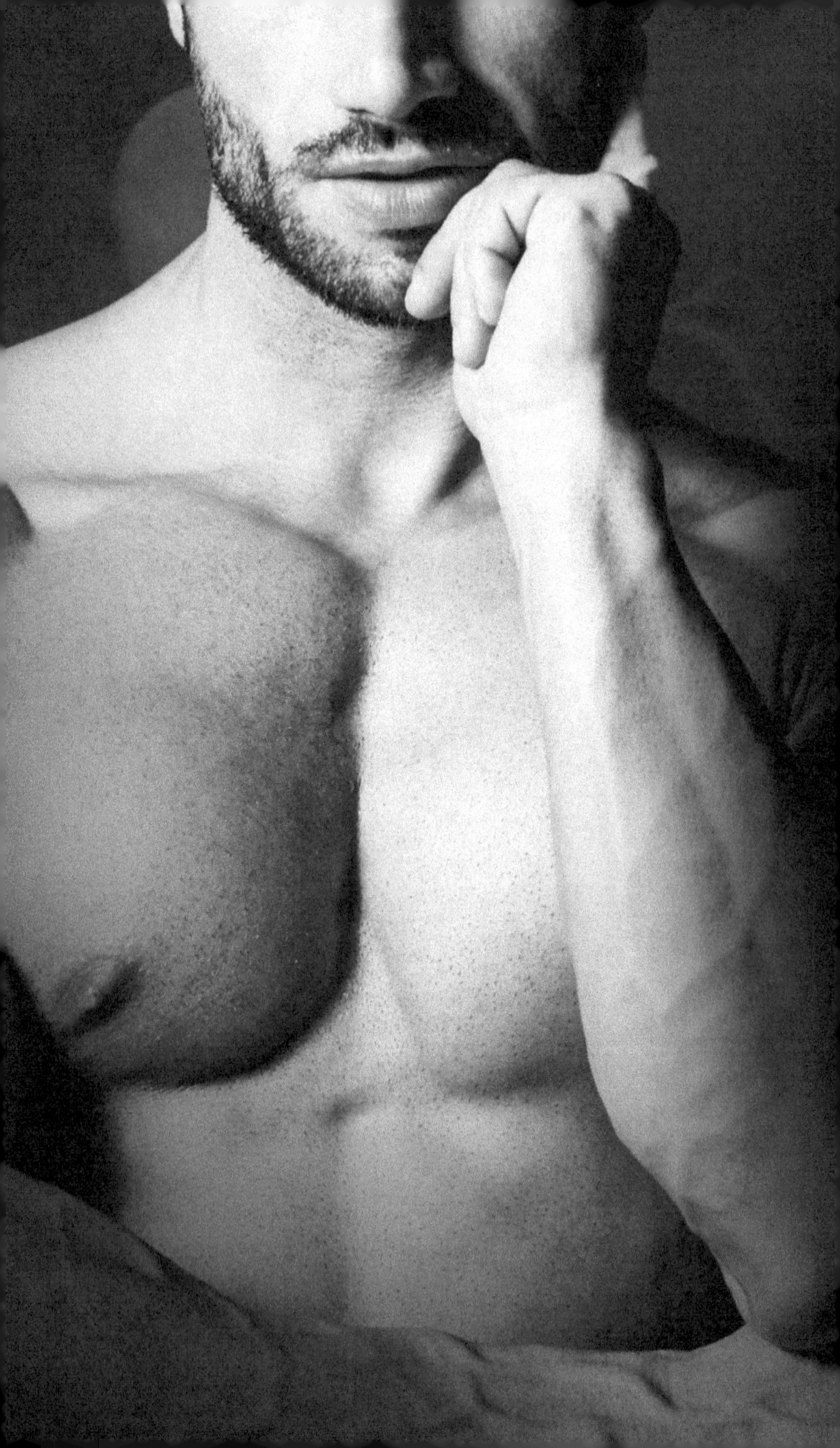

CHAPTER 12
ROMI

I'm sitting in Sullivan's living room, nestled comfortably in his oversized armchair with one leg draped over the side. The new mystery thriller I've been dying to read rests on my lap while Angus snores softly on the floor in front of me.

A soft, golden light spills across the room as the late afternoon sun drifts through the wide bay windows.

But my tranquility is short-lived as my phone rings shrilly, vibrating its way closer across the side table. Glancing at the screen, I see it's Yvette, my sister. Darn it. I've been meaning to call her, but I've never found the time. Frustration collides with curiosity as I finger-swipe to answer, pressing it to my ear.

"Hey, Vette," I greet, trying to figure out how to tell her I'm pretty much living with a man.

"Where are you?" comes her immediate demand,

bypassing any pleasantries or casual small talk. Her voice is edged with impatience and a hint of bewilderment.

Confused, I frown and glance around at my current setting. Angus lets out a little snore, still dreaming, blissfully unaware of the familial drama about to unfold. "What do you mean, 'Where am I?'" I counter, sounding more nonchalant than I feel.

"I'm at your apartment, Romi, standing here in your very much empty living room, and your landlady just told me you don't stay here very much." Her voice has that familiar edge of an older sister out to set the universe right.

Sinking further into the chair, I mentally brace myself for what's about to unfold. "Wait, what are you doing in Midnight Falls?"

"I'm here to surprise you!" my sister huffs, her exasperation punctuated by the unmistakable background noise of a low conversation with Ms. Viola, who's no doubt adding her own colorful commentary. "But it looks like you're the one with the surprise."

My initial bewilderment gives way to a prickling realization—I'm going to have to spill all the beans about Sullivan, the shift in my living situation, and the shift in my life to the last person I thought would just drop in.

"Okay, give me a minute," I say, trying to keep the mood light as I grapple with the quick change of plans. "I'm at Sullivan's. I'll text you his address."

"Sullivan? Who the freaking hell is Sullivan?" Her voice peaks with a mix of curiosity and thinly veiled alarm that only siblings can manage seamlessly.

"The man who owns my heart," I say, deciding there's no better time for full disclosure. Angus stirs at my feet, opening one eye as if assessing the approval of this reveal.

There's a pause on Yvette's end, and I grit my teeth waiting for the explosion. "Alright. I'll be there soon." Oof. It's even worse knowing I'll have to deal with the fallout in person.

After sending her Sullivan's address, I text Sullivan and let him know my sister is in town.

> ME
> Yvette showed up at Ms. Viola's unexpectedly.
>
> CAVEMAN
> What happened? Are you okay?
>
> ME
> She's on her way here now.
>
> CAVEMAN
> I'll be there in five minutes. I love you, little treat.
>
> ME
> I love you, too.

There's a whole gaggle of emotions swirling within me. Excitement, apprehension, and the looming drama of my sister's wrath all tangled up in a big ball of complicated yarn. I scratch Angus's ears contemplatively, his reassuring presence lessening the initial spike of anxiety.

"Here we go, buddy," I murmur, and he thumps his tail empathetically. "Hopefully, there's no bloodshed by the time today is over."

I hear Sullivan's monster truck pull up and breathe a sigh of relief. "Hey, little treat," he calls out, stepping into the living room. When he wraps his arms around me and pulls me close for his kiss, I forget about the coming storm and melt against him.

"I needed that," I respond when he pulls back. My heart nearly bursts from my chest as I attempt to rein in the nerves bubbling up inside me like a lava lamp. "Are you ready to deal with Hurricane Yvette?"

"Don't worry, little treat, everything will be fine," he assures me, but without skipping a beat, his eyes search mine, settling with familiarity and warmth. "I'll face anything to keep you. Even an overprotective older sister."

I chuckle, grateful for the levity he offers amidst my tempest of concerns. "You say that now, but wait until you meet her."

"Nothing will ever take you away from me. Don't worry, I'll win over your sister. I mean, how can she resist this adorable face?" He pastes the silliest expression on his handsome face, and I can't help but laugh at his antics.

Time flies and soon enough, there's the sound of a car pulling up the driveway. I peer out just in time to see Yvette step out, scrutinizing the surroundings with a hawk-like attention to detail. Sullivan takes my hand in his and opens the door as she reaches the porch.

"Yvette!" I announce, enveloping her in a quick hug before she has time to attack. Her sharp gaze shifts to Sullivan, evaluating, weighing as she hugs me back.

"So, this is Sullivan," Yvette states, eyes darting between us, assessing the situation.

Sullivan exchanges a polite handshake with a glaring Yvette.

"So..." Yvette pauses, releasing his hand with a half-smile that doesn't quite reach her eyes yet. "Why am I just finding out about you?"

Sullivan, bless him, offers a generous grin, the kind that signifies understanding. "I guess I've been keeping Romi so busy that she didn't have time to call you. I apologize for the confusion," he quips amiably. Angus, as always, nudges forward with animal intuition, offering Yvette his puppy-dog eyes full force.

Her tough gaze softens as she bends down to scratch his ears—inevitable chemistry easing into warmth, muttering a faint, "Aren't you a cute guy."

"Okay, here's what we're going to do," Yvette announces as she straightens, directing her focus back to Sullivan. You know it's serious when Angus isn't enough to distract. "I'm going to change my plans and stay in town for a few days to see for myself if my sister is okay with you. If I get any warning signs at all, I'll drag her back to Houston before you can blink."

"You're welcome to stay as long as you want, but no one is ever taking Romi away from me." Sullivan doesn't let my sister intimidate him. "I would never come between sisters, so you're going to have to work with me here."

"If you hurt my sister, I'll be your worst enemy." Yvette, a corporate attorney, isn't one to let a man get one over on her.

"You don't have to worry about that. Romi owns me, heart and soul. I would cut off my own arm before I hurt her," Sullivan declares, managing charm and sincerity in the unorthodox balance that makes his confidence so irresistible.

"We'll see." It surprises me to see my sister actually back down a little.

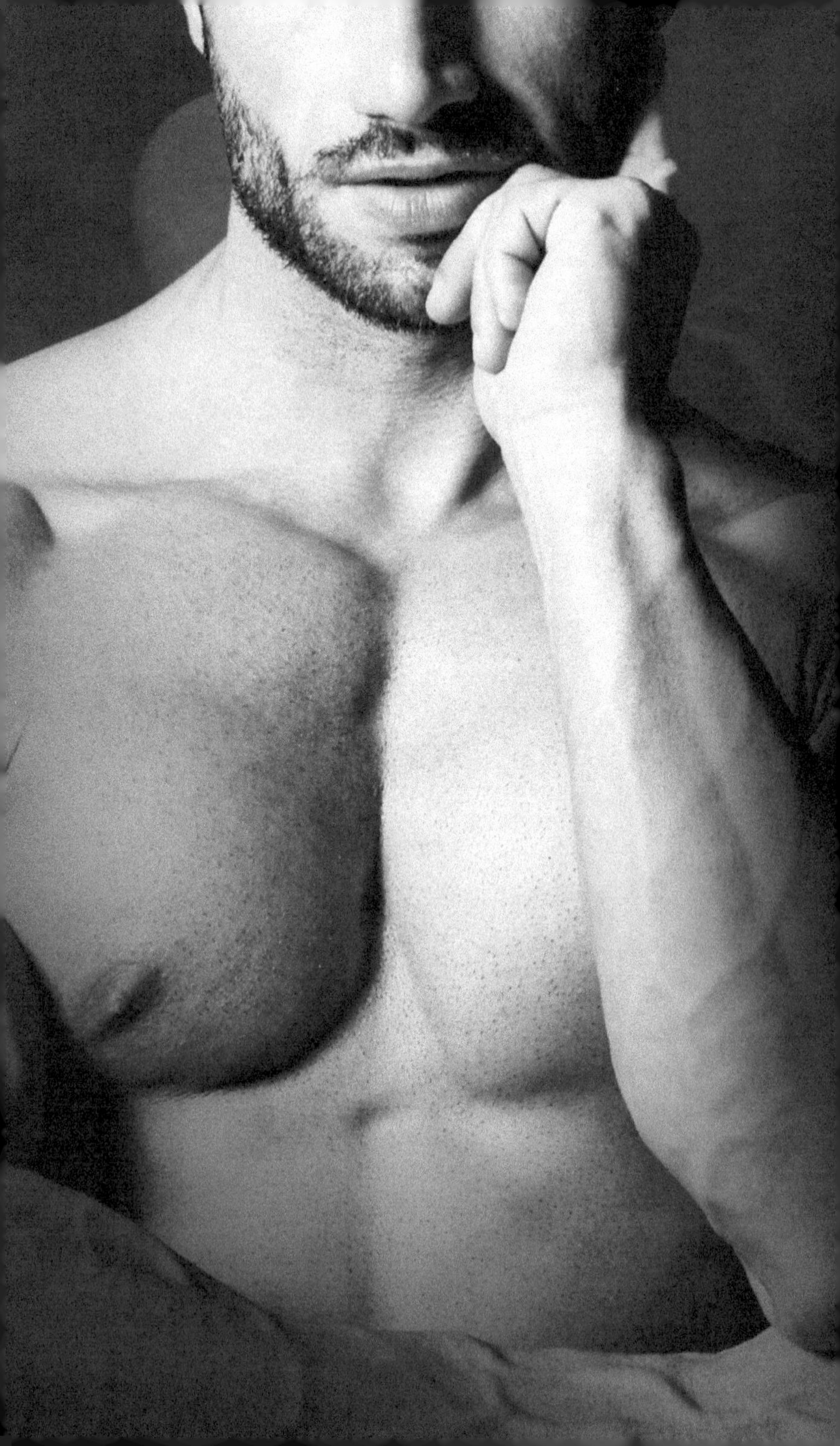

CHAPTER 13
SULLIVAN

Yvette is a ballbuster. That's the only way to put it. She has that fierce energy, the kind that makes a typical guy buckle a little under pressure with the threat of losing his family jewels hanging over his head. But not me. I've got a few tricks up my sleeve.

"I'll have a full investigation done on you by tomorrow morning, so you need to admit any secrets now," she declares the moment she steps into my living room, her hands on her hips, assessing her surroundings like a hawk sizing up its next meal. She's got that blend of sass and skepticism that says she means business.

"There aren't any skeletons in my closet. Well, except for Uncle Sinclair running naked through town with a tinfoil hat on his head," I reply with a reassuring grin, maybe a hint of mock seriousness to ease the impending storm brewing. Yvette's the epitome of a protective older sister, her eyes scanning like they're on a secret mission to measure my worthiness.

Her dark hair, which she has pulled back in a bun at the back of her head, adds an extra touch of seriousness to her demeanor. I can already predict our conversations will swing from playful to perilous. "That's a story I need to hear." A small smile flashes across her lips before she's able to stop it.

I shrug, unable to resist the urge to tease her a little. "You will at some point," I retort, raising an eyebrow with purposeful exaggeration. "Would you like something to drink?"

She snorts. "I could use something strong." But I can see it now—the tiniest flicker behind her eyes that hints at an unyielding acceptance of my attempts. "Very strong. It's been one of those weeks."

"What's going on?" Romi cuts in, and I notice the worry sketched across her expressive face.

"I'm dealing with a new attorney in the firm who's determined to make my life a living hell."

While the two sisters talk, I grab some steaks from the refrigerator and cook us a late lunch since Romi has to be at Trick or Treat early tonight for the Thirteen Nights of Halloween Costume Contest.

After our cozy meal on the back patio, Romi heads inside to grab a bottle of wine for Yvette.

"Listen, I'm not going to interfere with your relationship with my sister right now, but I have a few rules." Yvette turns to me, suddenly serious.

"Rules?" Feeling like I'm back in high school, I feign casual interest while internally bracing for whatever onslaught of protective siblinghood is coming my way. "Enlighten me."

"Rule Number One: No hurting her. Ever. I don't care how charming you think you are, or how many cute puppy dog eyes you flash. If you hurt her, I will make it my mission to become your worst nightmare." She meets my gaze with a fierceness that radiates through the air like heat waves, words heavy with the weight of older-sister authority. "You got that?"

I nod slowly, maintaining the easy charm. "We already covered this one. I will never hurt Romi."

Her demeanor softens a little, patience trailing behind that fire. "Good. Just know that I'll be watching."

"Duly noted."

Romi returns before we can get to any more of Yvette's rules, but I'm pretty sure I already know what they encompass—she wants the best for her sister and will do whatever it takes to make sure Romi gets it. My exact goal, too.

The atmosphere at Trick or Treat is electric as the Halloween Costume Contest kicks into full gear. I can practically feel the excitement buzzing off the walls, mingling with the spicy scents of pumpkin and cinnamon wafting through the room.

The bar is packed—pirates, witches, and zombies mingle as the night unfolds like a lifelike pop-up book full of colorful characters. I'm seated at a table with Yvette, who's still making me jump through hoops to prove I love her sister.

"So, you work for Midnight Industries." She's not really asking and I bet she already knows all about my family.

"That's right. I'm the head designer," I say, ready to defend my career choice. "My oldest brother made sure I got my Master's degree in Mechanical Engineering and had me interview and beat out other candidates for the position."

"He's smart. It's important to work for what you get and not have it handed to you." She taps her fingers against the table as she seems to weigh the phrase.

"Please don't ever tell Sterling you find him smart. I'll never hear the goddamn end of it."

"It can be our little secret." Yvette smirks, raising an eyebrow. "For now."

We both laugh, and I slant my head to survey the contest more thoroughly. Romi's up on stage, holding a microphone with such effortless charm she could probably sell ice to an Eskimo.

She smiles brightly at the crowd, egging them on to cheer for the participants, her enthusiasm infectious. I can't help but revel in how natural she looks up there, commanding attention yet bringing in a sense of playfulness.

"What the fuck?" I mutter to myself, leaning forward in my seat as I see the pirate push his way up on stage to stand right in front of Romi.

Just then, the pirate plants himself in front of her, leaning in way too close. "Ahoy, fair maiden! What's a beauty like you doin' in a place like this?" The microphone in her hand catches his drunk slurs.

Romi, ever the professional, slips a polite smile on her lips. "I'm just here to run this contest. Why don't you take a seat at the bar and check out the scary costumes?"

Before she can finish her sentence, the pirate cuts her off, lunging in and pulling her into his arms. My entire being ignites into a full-fledged fucking rage. The instinct to break the fucker in half surges like a tidal wave as I leap to my feet.

"Motherfucker!" I roar, pushing through the crowd, fueled by a rush of adrenaline. My caveman instincts go into overdrive as I march up to the stage, ready to confront the asshole who dared to touch my little treat.

In one swift motion, I yank the pirate back by the collar of his ridiculous shirt, pulling him away from Romi. "What the fuck do you think you're doing?" I glare at him, ready to tear his ass apart limb by limb.

He looks back at me, his bloodshot eyes holding an arrogant gleam. "What's it to you, buddy? I don't see a ring on her finger," he snaps, speaking like he fluently believes his logic excuses his crass behavior.

In that moment, fury and disbelief whirl together in a cyclone. "I'll fix that," I snarl. Reaching into my pocket where I've kept the ring I planned to give her tomorrow night, I turn my attention back to Romi, who's still trying to process what's happening. "Little treat," I begin, sweeping my eyes over her as I kneel slightly to present the ring, holding it forward like it's the literal light of stars. "I was planning to take you and your sister to Midnight Scares tomorrow night and propose on the new ride, but this asshole threw a monkey wrench into my plans. I love you more than anything in the world. Will you marry me?"

Romi's mouth drops open for a second, and I gauge her reaction, redirecting the energy swirling wildly around the room. I'm just as surprised as she is, really, but I've known since our first kiss that she's worth the leap I'm about to take. I notice Yvette standing on the side of the stage with tears in her eyes and realize I managed to win her over with my crazy display of love.

The pirate swells to his peak of indignation, foaming indignantly. "B-But—"

"It's your last goddamn chance to escape," I cut him off, giving him the chance to leave without my foot stuck up his ass while I pull Romi into my arms. The microphone squeaks when she drops it on the stage at our feet.

"Yes, I can't wait to be your wife, caveman," she whispers against my lips before kissing me for all the patrons in the bar to see. Having lived in this small town my entire life, I'm well acquainted with the town grapevine, and I have no doubt this display will be on everyone's lips tomorrow.

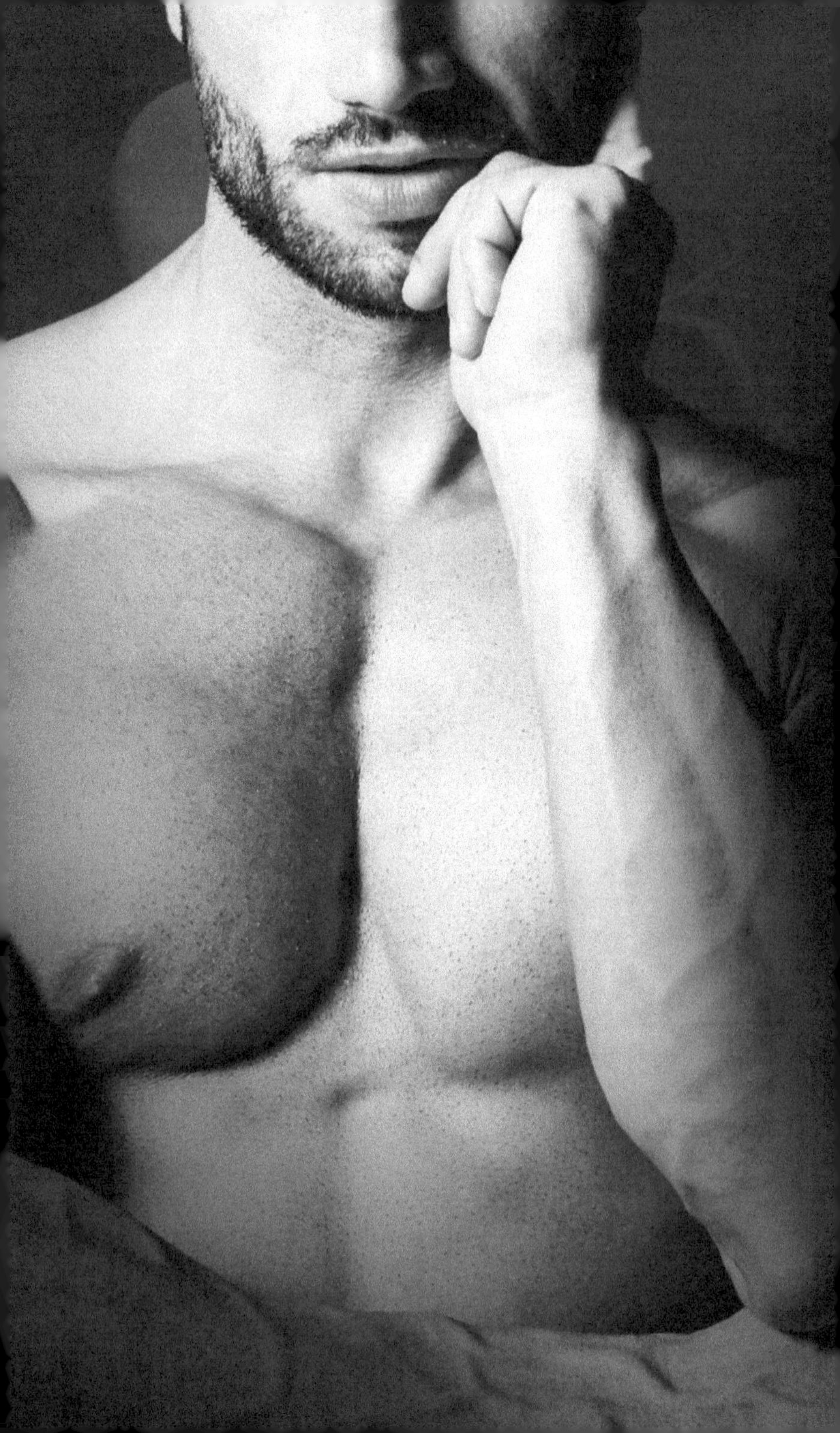

EPILOGUE
ROMI

Three months later

It's a misty morning in Midnight Falls, a few months after Sullivan and I took the plunge, quite literally, into the neon-lit wonderland of Las Vegas and came back as Mr. and Mrs. Midnight.

Since that evening of rhinestones and sequins, we've melded our lives together, leaping over any hurdles and roadblocks that threatened our cozy union.

My things are now scattered in strategically chaotic harmony throughout our house, and Angus has gotten accustomed to his new bed next to the fireplace in our room. He fought the change in sleeping arrangements for a few days, but the new treats I found online helped change his mind.

Tony wasn't too enthused when I asked to work part-time hours in the club and do the paperwork from home, but my boss finally decided he could live with that. Especially if it keeps my powerful husband happy.

Yvette, seeing an opportunity to escape the new attorney who was making her life hell, opened her firm in nearby Silver Spoon Falls. The small town a few miles away is known for its billionaire residents, lavish mansions, and special water that is rumored to cause love-at-first-sight unions.

Surprisingly enough, Midnight Industries became her first bigwig client, ensuring her venture hit the ground running. I couldn't be prouder, though let's face it; Sullivan's brothers are probably thrilled to have an ally as capable as Yvette in their corner.

Today, I'm grappling with my own little secret. I've been feeling under the weather every morning this past week, and I'm pretty sure our lack of birth control use is the reason for it. To verify my suspicions, I dig out the pregnancy test I hid under the bathroom counter a few days ago.

After taking a few minutes to calm my frazzled nerves, I pee on the stick and wait to see if our little world is about to do a one-eighty. Two minutes later, my suspicions are confirmed, and I couldn't be happier.

I'm practically vibrating with excitement and decide to distract myself by taking Angus for our daily walk. He seems to understand things more deeply than any human I've met, and the exercise will do us both some good.

As we wander through the familiar trail leading to the

pond on the back of our property, I secretly confide in Angus how his world is about to change.

"You're going to be a big brother, Angus," I murmur during our usual route, my words hanging in the crisp morning air like bubbles waiting to pop. He looks up at me with those soulful eyes and wagging tail, as if he could sense the change long before my brain caught up.

Returning home, I realize I need to find a creative way to share my little secret with Sullivan. Curling up on the couch, I plot my reveal with Angus by my side, the silent vault keeper of secrets. When an idea pops into my mind, I hop up and grab my laptop, hoping to find a t-shirt shop in the area.

Two hours later, a delivery man drops off my special-order Angus-sized t-shirt that reads, *I'm the Big Brother*. I call in a few favors and get Adam, Sterling's assistant, to let me know when Sullivan leaves for the day so I'll be ready for our big reveal.

After I receive Adam's text, I coax Angus into donning his new attire. He gives me a look that conveys I'm going to need to buy some more of those fancy treats for him before sitting like a good boy at the door to wait for Sullivan.

Sullivan, coming home from a day engrossed in Midnight Industries meetings and maintenance, barely steps through the door before Angus bounds toward him with unreserved enthusiasm. I'm watching from the kitchen, my heart pounding with happiness and excitement.

"Hey, buddy! What've you got there?" Sullivan laughs, crouching to greet Angus. The moment his eyes alight on the text, I hear his long indrawn breath.

"Surprise!" I step next to them.

Sullivan jumps to his feet and pulls me into his arms before I'm able to take a breath. "I fucking love you, little treat."

"You aren't upset that we aren't going to be alone for long?" I have to be sure. He's been teasing about knocking me up, but we've never really discussed having children.

"Upset?" He stares down at me with wide eyes before leaning down to whisper against my lips, "I've been trying my hardest to knock your little ass up since the first time I touched your gorgeous body."

Happiness bursts through me as I laugh. "Then I guess your little swimmers did their job."

"About fucking time." Sullivan scoops me up into his arms and heads straight for our bedroom. "We have to get this show on the road if we're going to have our six or seven kids before we get too old."

"Six or seven?" We haven't really discussed the number of kids we each want, and this is the first time I've heard Sullivan's hopes.

"At least." He laughs and drops me on the bed, and I stare up at him with happiness and love shining from my eyes.

"Why don't we start with one baby and see how that

goes, and then we can renegotiate?" I suggest as I pull my t-shirt off over my head.

"Anything for you, little treat," he growls and steps back to pull off his polo shirt. As he drops it to the ground at his feet, I realize I'm one lucky lady. I have the best husband in the world, a wonderful family, and a job I love. Life couldn't get any better than this.

THE END OF *MIDNIGHT Treat*

Related Stories

RELATED STORIES

SILVER SPOON SINGLE SERVE

dating the billionaire

LONI NICHOLE

RELATED STORIES

Hot Water

LONI NICHOLE

SUBSCRIBE TO MY NEWSLETTER

GET HOW TO LOVE A HEARTBREAKER WHEN YOU SUBSCRIBE TO MY NEWSLETTER

Loni Ree Romance Newsletter

BUY PAPERBACKS AND EBOOKS

DID YOU KNOW YOU CAN BUY SIGNED PAPERBACKS AND HARDCOVERS PLUS SOME OF MY EBOOKS DIRECTLY FROM ME.

www.lonireeromance.com

JOIN MY READER'S GROUP
FIND OUT ABOUT MY NEW RELEASES, SALES AND OTHER PROMOTIONS.

Facebook Group (Hot Heroes and Happy Endings)

ABOUT THE AUTHOR

LONI Ree

CURVY, FLIRTY AND A LITTLE BIT DIRTY

USA Today Bestselling Author Loni Ree is a busy mom of six who spends her free time writing steamy stories about over the top heroes who find the right curvy woman to tame them. Her stories are a little over the top because she believes reading should be an escape from real life.

She lives in the Midwest with her wonderful husband, the last child at home, and a zoo of animals, including Beau, her beloved French Bulldog.

Loni also has an alternate pen name L. Ree. If you like clean, sweet romance, check out her L. Ree books.

Website: Hotheroesandhea.com
https://linktr.ee/loniree19

Loni Ree
xoxo

- facebook.com/lonireeromance
- instagram.com/lonireeromance
- amazon.com/author/loniree
- bookbub.com/authors/loni-ree
- goodreads.com/LoniRee

ALSO BY LONI REE

Find an updated list of my books on my website:

https://www.hotheroesandhea.com/